TRAPPED

David Buckalew could clearly see both ends of the pass. When the Indians came against them it would probably be from the south end. He brought the spyglass to his eye and searched in that direction. Eventually he caught a flutter of movement to the north. He blinked and looked again. Because of the distance, the image jumped and danced. He knelt to brace the telescope against a boulder and slowly swung the end around until he could focus on what he had seen.

"Yankees!" he said aloud and in surprise. "A bunch of them ridin' straight into the pass."

He knew suddenly why the Indians hadn't yet bothered the little Texas troop huddled behind their miserable pile of rocks. They had easier prey to trap, and more of them.

But when they were finished with the Yankees, the Indians would turn on Buckalew's men, and that would be the inglorious finish to this dirty little campaign.

Other books by Elmer Kelton

Long Way to Texas

Elmer Kelton

BANTAM BOOKS

NEW YORK · TORONTO · LONDON · SYDNEY · AUCKLAND

All of the characters in this book are fictitious, and any
resemblance to actual persons,
living or dead, is purely coincidental.

This edition contains the complete text
of the original hardcover edition.
NOT ONE WORD HAS BEEN OMITTED.

LONG WAY TO TEXAS
A Bantam Book / published by arrangement with
Doubleday

PRINTING HISTORY
Doubleday edition published August 1976
Bantam edition / February 1987
2 printings through May 1990

This book was first published under Elmer Kelton's pseudonym of
Lee McElroy

ISBN 0-553-26449-4

Published simultaneously in the United States and Canada

Bantam Books are published by Bantam Books, a division of Bantam
Doubleday Dell Publishing Group, Inc. Its trademark, consisting of the
words "Bantam Books" and the portrayal of a rooster, is Registered in U.S.
Patent and Trademark Office and in other countries. Marca Registrada.
Bantam Books, 666 Fifth Avenue, New York, New York 10103.

PRINTED IN THE UNITED STATES OF AMERICA

O   0 9 8 7 6 5 4 3 2

Long Way to Texas

1

Death, when it finally came, would be savage and swift. But the waiting seemed eternal. For more than two hours Lieutenant David Buckalew had huddled with his nineteen tired and ragged men in this vulnerable hilltop redoubt and had wondered when the Indians would come shrieking up that barren slope to take them.

What in the hell were they waiting for?

A chilly wind swept across the low circle of hastily piled rocks. Buckalew fastened the three remaining buttons of his gray coat, the only remnant of a uniform that had been new and proud a few months ago in Texas. The wind searched its way through a long rent beneath his right arm. He held the arm against his body and shivered. He wondered if April was really that cold or if the chill came from within.

This, he thought bitterly, was an unfitting place for twenty men from Texas to die, and an unfitting way. They had come to an unfamiliar land to fight a just and honorable war against the Union Army, not to be cut to ribbons by a band of Indians with whom they had no quarrel, whose tribe they didn't even know.

The hard-used Texans had come upon the warriors while working their way along the fringe of scrub pine timber, moving southward through the mountains of eastern New Mexico. The confrontation had surprised the Indians as much as the Texans. The Indians had brought their horses to a sudden halt and gazed uncertainly at the white men across the space of perhaps a hundred yards. There had been at least thirty of them, and probably nearer forty. The number had been growing since. Buckalew had seen additional warriors trailing in.

Perhaps that indicated a respect of sorts. He hadn't seen much respect lately. Since he had been assigned to this unit against his will and theirs, he had encountered difficulty in getting the men to obey his orders, or even listen to him. But when they faced the Indians he had merely pointed toward the top of this hill. He had had to put spurs to his big brown horse to keep from being left behind. There had been stragglers earlier along the trail, but there were none on this hurried climb. The Indians had followed along, shouting challenges but firing no shots.

At the top of the hill the men had quickly, and without directions, set about building what fortification they could. They stacked rocks into a rough circular wall as a shield.

That the Indians could sweep up that hillside and wipe them out, David Buckalew had no doubt. But it wouldn't be done cheaply or easily.

The men had tried to dig down behind the crude wall but made no headway in the stony ground, for they had no real tools for the job. For the twentieth time he expanded his spyglass to full length with cold-sweaty hands and took a long sweeping look downhill. For some time he had watched Indians working in and out of a narrow pass. Now he saw little movement.

If they'd caught us in there, we'd be dead already, he thought, shivering. Weighing heavily upon him was the hard realization that he had almost led the men into that pass. He hadn't given Indians a thought at the time—he had seen no need to—and he had been reasonably sure no Yankee pursuit had passed them to set up an ambush. But solid old Sergeant Noley Mitchell had saved him from that fatal mistake. He had suggested they climb up over the rough side of the hill. David had seen no need for it, but the men started to follow Mitchell's suggestion anyway. There had been nothing left for the lieutenant to do but make it an order and salvage whatever dignity he might from a situation already out of his hands.

It had been clear from the start that although David Buckalew had the commission, Noley Mitchell had the men.

Mitchell had evidenced no malice that David could see as he watched the men climbing the hill. He said simply, "Call it a notion, Davey."

That was the way it had been since he had been assigned to this unit in Albuquerque: *Davey*. Not *Lieutenant*, not *Sir*, but just *Davey* to Noley Mitchell, as if David were some kid, not a man already in his twenties. It was little wonder the rest of the men didn't respect his rank.

Mitchell had said as they started bringing up the rear, "I just don't like gettin' caught in tight, narrow places. Goes back to ridin' a rough horse through a narrow gate when I was a boy and crushin' my leg against the post. I never forgot it, though it was a long time ago." It had indeed been a long time, because Noley Mitchell was twice David's age, and perhaps a bit more. In deference to that age, David gave him the benefit of many nagging doubts.

Now that Mitchell had been proven right about their not going through the pass, David knew the men were thinking and perhaps even saying among themselves that it was the old sergeant—not the young lieutenant—who had saved them from dying in it. Of course it had been only a temporary reprieve, for it looked very likely that they would die on the hilltop instead.

He could clearly see both ends of the pass. When the Indians came against them it would probably be from the south end. He kept bringing the spyglass to his eye and searching in that direction. Eventually he caught a flutter of movement to the north. He blinked and looked again. Because of the distance, the image jumped and danced. He knelt to brace the telescope against a boulder and very slowly swung the end around until he could focus on what he had seen.

"Yankees!" he said aloud and in surprise. "A bunch of them, ridin' straight into the pass."

He knew suddenly why the Indians hadn't yet bothered the little Texas group huddled behind their miserable pile of rocks. They had easier prey to trap, and more of them.

Sergeant Mitchell, kneeling down carefully on stiff knees, could see little with his naked eyes. David judged that he probably needed spectacles. "Let me have the glass a minute, Davey."

David grunted. Rank meant no more to Mitchell—or to the rest of these men—than it meant to a packmule. Mentally they were civilians, and they would never be anything else. So, for that matter, was David. But at least he *tried* to be a soldier. Lately he felt he was the only one left who did.

Mitchell growled about his difficulty in bringing the glass to bear on the target. He rubbed a ham-sized fist over his eye and tried again. "Yep, it's bluebellies."

David said, "They've taken the pressure off of us for now. Might be a good time for us to clear out."

Mitchell ran stubby fingers through a gray-salted two-inch tangle of beard coarse as porcupine quills and shook his head. "They'd just come after us later, if they're of a mind to. Where they caught us might not be half as good as the place we've got right here, button."

Mitchell had a Texan's way of referring to any young person as *button*, no matter how much military rank he might carry. Texans stood in awe of few things, and certainly not the gold bars of a second lieutenant. David understood that Mitchell had served many years as sheriff in some county south of Austin. Nothing fazed him much.

The men had heard Mitchell's comment. If David ordered them to go, most would probably stay here anyway. He saved himself the humiliation.

The chilly wind kept finding its way through the split seams of the gray coat his mother had made for him. The piping, stitched with great hopes by loving hands, hung loose and useless. The left sleeve showed a dark stain, and a hole that had been carelessly darned by male hands unused to needle and thread. David let his mind run back to a time when it was new, to that grand marshaling day in San Antonio, a fine day of fiery speeches and patriotism. With the stirring words still echoing in their minds, an intrepid band of Texas Confederates had started westward on a march meant to carry them all the way to the Pacific.

This was the Territory of New Mexico in April of 1862. The Civil War had pitted white man against white man, and red men against them all. It had been less than a year since flamboyant Captain John R. Baylor, famed for his exploits as a Texas Ranger, had recruited his Second Texas Mounted Rifles in San Antonio and had led them across the desert to begin the conquest of the Western territories for the greater glory of the Confederacy. It had seemed a splendid idea at the time, and to David it still did. The Union forts in New Mexico and Arizona were poorly defended. A preponderance of their officers and a fair percentage of their enlisted men had been Southerners who had resigned at the outset of the war. They had returned to their homes to help raise an army for the Confederacy, leaving their former posts short on men and shorter on leadership. Moreover, because these forts were so far from the East and adjoined on one side by Confederate Texas, they were virtually isolated. They were considered beyond help if any concerted effort were made against them.

Behind Baylor's fast-moving cavalry had moved the huge but slower brigade of Henry Hopkins Sibley, late of the Union Army post in Santa Fe, now a general for Jefferson Davis. He knew the western military installations by virtue of his service there; he knew the weak points of every one. The Texans had first taken Fort Bliss at Paso del Norte without bloodshed. Poorly equipped from the standpoint of arms, and mostly dressed in civilian clothes because nobody had the time or the material to supply proper uniforms, the Texas force had overcome distance and heat and cold and hunger through eight hard months on alien ground. They had marched from one victory to another, plucking Union apples from the tree . . . Fort Fillmore, San Augustine Springs, Valverde. They had raised the Texas flag over Albuquerque and ancient Santa Fe.

Total victory had seemed in easy reach, for the Arizona side of the Territory presented no challenge. Tucson was in Confederate hands. Beyond Arizona lay California, ripe for the taking. Its goldfields would finance the Confederacy's armed might. Its great open seacoast would provide an outlet to the world, an outlet so huge no Union blockade could seal it.

With all that in Confederate hands, how long could the gangling Abe Lincoln and his upstart Yankee Congress continue to deny the Southern states their right to secede from the Union, their right to govern themselves in a new and sovereign nation?

It had been a daring plan, conceived in the first flush of Texan euphoria at the outbreak of the war and sustained by the ease of victory over one weakened Union post after another.

But the Texans had considered New Mexico isolated because it was so far from the Union East. They had not taken into account that help might come from the west and north. They had only dimly known about the column of Union volunteers who had marched out of California to challenge the great desert, and of another which had ventured across the Rocky Mountains of Colorado and down through the San Luis Valley.

Disaster had come suddenly. On the twenty-seventh day of March the Confederate volunteers and the Union volunteers had slammed together at Glorieta. Badly overextended, sustaining themselves in a hostile land by supply lines which stretched hundreds of miles back into Texas, the Confederates were vulnerable to any interruption in these supplies. "Preacher" Chivington's Colorado men caught a vital ammunition train in the middle of Apache Canyon and destroyed it without mercy.

That great column of black smoke had cast a fatal shadow across the Confederate dream of Western conquest. The taste of victory turned to ashes in Texans' mouths. Splintered into dozens of disorganized and almost leaderless groups scattered over half of New Mexico and all of hell, short on ammunition and shorter on food, they had little choice except to retreat south under the pressure of determined Union pursuit, to try to reach Texas and hope the Californians and the Coloradans wouldn't hound them all the way back to San Antonio.

On the map, if David had had one, Texas lay a relatively few miles directly to the east. But that part was as hostile as New Mexico, for it was still firmly in Indian hands. The maps left the Panhandle region of Texas almost a total blank, marked only as "unknown Indian land." Beyond the cap rock stretched the great staked plains, familiar only to Comanche and Kiowa and to a relative handful of Indian traders operating out of eastern New Mexico. No white men known to the Texans had ever traversed it, had ever seen its hidden watering places or traced out its rivers and streams, had ever traveled the dim trails stretching across that vast and markless tableland of grass.

To David Buckalew and his men, and to other scattered units like them, the real Texas lay to the south. If they could ever reach Fort Bliss, they could then strike eastward along the military, immigrant and stagecoach road which would lead them to the Pecos, to the Conchos, and eventually to the safe and settled lands just west of San Antonio.

But it was a long way to Bliss, and Union scouting parties had been doing their best to seek them out and cut them to pieces. To the Yankees this was insurance against the Texans' ever again trying to carry the war across the Western territories. David's group was a remnant of many which had been ordered to lag behind and fight a rearguard action, to delay Union pursuit long enough so that the larger bodies of men, particularly the walking infantry, could have a long head start.

David watched the mirror flashes as the Indians talked to each other across the near end of the pass. He could no longer see the Union troops; they had moved into the trap. The gunfire started, echoing off the ragged mountain walls. David shivered. He was too far away to hear the shouts and the screams with his ears, but he heard them in his mind. Through the glass he saw riderless horses galloping out of the pass, some on this side, some going back through the far end. He saw two men spurring desperately and watched the mounted pursuit that inevitably caught up. He saw the men fall, and the Indians jump down around them.

He had seen much of death in New Mexico, but he had never managed to harden himself against the coldness that settled in the bottom of his stomach. The gunfire became scattered. Finally it stopped altogether. He licked his dry and wind-chapped lips as he trained the spyglass on the near opening of the defile. At last he saw Indians begin to spill out of it. He could count at least fifty; there might have been more. Many led extra horses that he knew carried cavalry saddles.

The Indians moved toward the hill where the Texans crouched or lay waiting in dread, gripping their rifles. A young soldier who had never shaved out of necessity recited the Lord's Prayer over and over.

At length a dark-stubbled, hawk-featured man said irritably, "Richey, I wisht you'd shut up."

Pete Richey glanced at Luther Lusk with stricken eyes. "Luther, I'm just askin' the Lord to help us."

"If He didn't hear you the first time, He ain't listenin'. You're makin' me almighty nervous."

David said, "Let him alone. A little prayin' a long time ago mightn't of hurt *you* any."

"He'd do better to save his breath for the fight."

David looked at the boy, a seventeen-year-old farm lad who had lied about his age to get into the volunteers, and lately had had ample cause to regret it. "You go on with it, Richey, if you want to."

Pete Richey gave David a grateful look, then glanced uneasily at Luther Lusk. For a moment David thought he might finally have made a friend. But Richey was overawed by the frontiersman Lusk, too much to challenge him. He turned back to his rifle. His lips moved again, but his prayer was silent.

David frowned at Lusk, a thick-set man wearing a fancy Mexican-style coat over a tattered homespun cotton shirt. Lusk had appropriated the coat out of a store after beating up the Mexican storekeeper, a man burly enough to present him a challenge. He had defended himself on the grounds that the man had a Union flag draped on the wall, and besides that, his father had probably fought in the battle of the Alamo. If he hadn't, he probably was friends with somebody who had. Nothing came of the incident except an admonishment from higher officers. From what David had seen, Lusk was something of a wild man. Admonishing a wild man was like using a willow switch against a bear.

"Sergeant," David said to Noley Mitchell, "you'd better give Lusk his rifle. He'll need it directly."

He had taken the trooper's rifle after a set-to three days ago. David's orders had been to retreat gradually, harassing the Union troops wherever it was practical without undue risk to his men, slowing down the Union advance. He had orders not to take suicidal risks, but to get his small command back to Texas intact and safe if he possibly could. He had been hitting small Union details from ambush, then running before they had time to react.

They had sighted a Union force much too large for them. Luther Lusk had wanted to charge it anyway and "get in one more good lick against them damnyankee bastards before we turn tail and run." David had seen it as a clear case of suicide and had forbidden it.

"I'll go by myself, by God!" Lusk had shouted angrily. "If there's any man here with sand, he'll go with me."

David had seen fit to club Lusk over the head with the barrel of a pistol and tie him to his saddle. He reasoned that he had saved not only Lusk's life but those of the other men.

The troop as a whole was not keen on following Lusk into a moment of glory and an eternity of sleep. Nevertheless, their sympathies were clearly with him. David had made no friends by his rough but effective method of stopping Luther Lusk. He kept telling himself he shouldn't worry about it. These were not the men with whom he had campaigned through most of his time in New Mexico; he had recently been assigned to them against their will and his own. His original outfit had been badly shot to pieces, David himself falling among the wounded. These volunteers had lost their lieutenant, elected by them back home and willingly followed by them until his death. Instead of allowing them to elect another of their own choice, the higher-ups had chosen to impose upon them this stranger, a green young officer from the old and peaceful Stephen F. Austin colony way back in what was now considered East Texas. What could a young upstart like that know of battle? There hadn't been anything bigger than a crossroads fistfight down in that section for at least twenty years.

Lusk grasped the rifle as Mitchell extended it to him. He jerked it roughly from the sergeant's hands and said caustically to David, "Thank you, Lieutenant, for all your generosity. I thought you was fixin' to make me throw rocks at them."

"When this is over," David said evenly, "that rifle goes back to Sergeant Mitchell."

"When this is over," Lusk replied in a cold voice, "this rifle will go to some redskin. You know it and I know it."

One Indian rode out in advance of the others. He stopped a hundred yards short of the hilltop. He was in easy range, but nobody shot at him. The warrior waved a rifle and began to yell. The wind was blowing the wrong direction for David and the others to hear him. They would not have understood the words anyway.

Lusk said bitterly, "Go out there and arrest him, Buckalew."

Several more Indians moved up even with the first one. They waved muskets and some newly captured Yankee rifles. Fresh scalps dangled from the firearms. David knew little of sign language, but he understood the more graphic gestures.

Suddenly the Indians wheeled their horses around and rode away, shouting victory to the mountains, carrying their trophies with them.

David watched in disbelief. After a minute he stood up, his mouth hanging open. He studied the mountains with the spyglass, hunting for a sign of other Indians lying in wait.

Young Richey prayed again, this time giving thanks.

David knew little about Indians. He had been a boy when the last raid occurred in Hopeful Valley. He had heard many stories and doubted half of them. He distrusted people who claimed to know all about Indians, because his father said such people were all talk. He glanced at Mitchell, who had never made such a claim. "What do you make of it, Sergeant?"

Mitchell replied in a gravel-voiced drawl. "I fought Indians down home in the wild old days. All I ever learned for sure was that you never do know. They hunt people for sport, the way me and you would hunt a deer when we wasn't really hungry. When they've satisfied their appetite they're ready to go off and celebrate. Maybe tomorrow they'll get the notion to come lookin' for us. But today it looks like they've had glory enough."

Luther Lusk pushed to his feet and headed for his horse. "Well, I come here to fight Yankees; I ain't lost no Indians."

"Lusk!" David shouted. "You halt right there. You give that rifle back to Sergeant Mitchell."

Lusk turned on his heel. For a long moment the big man's hawk eyes glared at the officer, challenging him. The muzzle was pointed vaguely in David's direction. The temptation showed strongly in his face.

"What if I choose to do otherwise?"

David said tensely, "Then I'll kill you!" It was an empty statement, for he knew he wouldn't. But he stood and bluffed because he had already lost too much ground with these men.

Lusk had all the advantage, if he chose to use it. Chances were small that he would ever be prosecuted back in Texas for something done here in the mountains of New Mexico. But in a moment he handed the rifle to Mitchell. "Hell, let some Indian kill him; then nobody'll stretch *my* neck."

David said, "Don't anybody rush. We'll leave here with order."

"Order?" Lusk was incredulous. "What does order mean to an Indian? If we want to live to fight more Yankees, we'd better forget about order and get the hell away from this place."

David's back was rigid. "You seem to've forgotten how it was the day we all rode out of San Antonio. Like as not you were drunk. But *I* remember. We rode out of there proud. Well, we've been beaten, but we're not whipped. We won't go back to Texas *lookin'* whipped." He knew most of the men just wanted to leave there. He would not have admitted it, but his own britches were burning him. "Mount up."

That was another order he had to give but once. The men began edging their horses south, but David motioned for them to follow him. He moved down the east side of the hill toward the pass.

Noley Mitchell spurred up beside him. "I don't mean to question your judgment, button, but Texas is yonderway."

"Those Yankees might've brought somethin' we can use."

"Davey, you can bet them Indians picked up every gun, every knife, every cartridge."

"But maybe not all the rations. Indian tastes don't run to military issue. And maybe we'll find some canteens. For what's ahead of us, we can use every water container we can find."

Mitchell would have argued further, but David showed no disposition to listen. His eyes were set firmly on the pass, and the old lawman took that sign for what it was. He rode quietly, glancing over his broad shoulder to be sure everybody was coming.

David wanted to look back but feared that could be taken as a sign of doubt. He held the lead, sitting straight in the saddle the way his father had taught him. Joshua Buckalew had been one of the early "Texians," those who came before the revolution. He emigrated from Tennessee in 1830, taking up land in Austin's colony, fighting in the revolt against Santa Anna and Mexico. He had been a survivor of the massacre at Goliad and had found his way to Sam Houston's army in time for the final victory at San Jacinto.

Joshua Buckalew had been a soldier, a hard man for a son to follow in the eyes of the people in Hopeful Valley, and those elsewhere who had ever known Joshua.

David's father had never expressed pride in the battles he had fought; on the contrary, he hated even to talk about them. But other people talked, and exaggerated. Joshua Buckalew was a reluctant hero in the land where he had chosen to live out his life. People expected much from his son. That was why David had been elected lieutenant of the Hopeful Valley volunteers . . . not for himself but because of his father.

Up to now, David had to consider himself a failure. It was a hard thing to be a son of Joshua Buckalew and still be a failure.

Joshua hadn't said much as David had prepared to ride away to San Antonio with the valley's other recruits. "There's a lot you ain't seen yet, and you've got a lot to learn about life," he had cautioned, his eyes glazed. "You'll find a lot of it ain't the way you expect it to be, and sure not like people say. You'll find a lot that ain't just and fair. But set yourself straight and ride always in the service of the Lord. You'll owe no man an apology if you do the best that's in you."

The Lord had precious little to do with this *war,* David thought with some bitterness. There had been a certain amount of public praying at the muster in San Antonio, and calls upon the Deity for His guidance in the righteous campaign. But it had not taken David long to decide that the Lord had no great leaning to either side. He had let both suffer horribly, and the suffering was far from over.

The speeches and the music had been fine, and the flags had waved gallantly as they had set out upon the first long march. But shortly after coming into New Mexico he had watched a man die screaming, trying to hold his shattered guts in place.

There had been no music then.

Now David was increasingly certain that all this suffering had been for nothing. Wasted were all those hard miles they had fought, all those days they had ridden until their tailbones were numb and their dry tongues stuck to the roofs of their mouths. All those men who had died, all those men who had gone home maimed for the rest of their lives . . . they had done it for nothing. The campaign was lost.

It hadn't been what he had expected. It was hell being a soldier.

A dull ache worked through his shoulder, a reminder of the price he himself had paid. The wound had never completely healed; he was not sure it ever would. They had pulled him out of the makeshift military hospital in Albuquerque too soon, for they had badly needed officers. It had been his doubly bad luck that he was assigned to this outfit which didn't want him. Had the men been allowed an election, David did not doubt that they would have chosen Noley Mitchell, and he would be the one leading them back to Texas.

The irony was that he knew the old lawman would probably do a better job of it.

Leadership had been an easy thing in those early months of the war. All the Hopeful Valley men were his friends, and all knew what needed to be done. He didn't have to give orders. Being an officer was more an honor than a responsibility. It was no great challenge to lead when they were winning, and winning easily.

The crisis of leadership came now, when they were losing. This was the true test. Ever since he had been with this outfit, David Buckalew had fallen short.

God, for one more chance!

Before riding down into the pass he sent Noley Mitchell up on one side of it and a Mexican trooper named Fermin Hernandez up on the other to scout for Indians. David had never been comfortable about the Mexican; it was an old ingrained prejudice from his part of the country, where Anglos and Mexicans had fought two official wars and many unofficial ones. Yet he had found that Hernandez possessed the best eyesight of any man in the outfit. The Mexican could not read words written on a page, but he could read tracks on the ground and describe in considerable detail the circumstances of their making. He could see riders a mile away and tell if they were soldiers or Indians or what. He was useful as an interpreter, too, for David's knowledge of Spanish was rudimentary at best, geared to the limited vocabulary he had needed in his chosen trade, the buying, training and selling of horses and mules.

Hernandez gave the "clear" sign, and a moment later Mitchell did likewise. David left half the men posted in the mouth of the pass to stand guard. He took the others in to look over the battleground.

Battleground was not exactly the word for it. It had been more slaughter than battle. The blueclad troops had had little chance to fight back. The Indians had been well hidden in the rocks on either side and presented little target. The Union soldiers lay scattered along the pass, heaped like bloody rag dolls, scalped and mutilated. David's stomach started to turn, and he shut his eyes for a moment until the feeling passed.

At a glance he knew the Indians had taken all guns and ammunition; he had expected that. He came upon a dead packmule. The Indians had ripped the pack off, looking for anything they could use. David motioned to the youth

Richey to go through what was left. He saw a dead horse with the saddle still on, and a canteen tied to it.

He glanced behind him at a farm lad named Ivy, who had always been eager but was considered by the others as a bit slow in his thinking. "Ivy, you been needin' a better saddle. Get somebody to help you take that one."

Ivy was dubious. "There's blood on it, Lieutenant."

"It'll wear off."

David turned away, then stopped abruptly. Staring up toward him with sightless eyes was a man wearing captain's bars on a bullet-torn, faded-blue uniform. David dismounted. Kneeling, he shuddered a little as his fingers lightly touched the man's face and closed the dulled eyes. He began going through the pockets. There might be papers.

Inside the coat he found an envelope, its corner stained a sticky red. As he opened it he heard a noise behind him. A frontier trapper named Jake Calvin was going through the pockets of the Union soldiers nearby.

"Calvin!"

Calvin looked up, startled. "You say somethin', Buckalew?" He had made his living with a skinning knife. Dead things brought him no dread.

"Don't you draw the line at robbin' bodies?"

"Who's robbin'? I'm just salvagin', same as you."

"I'm lookin' for dispatches, orders . . . nothin' else."

"And I'm just lookin' for tobacco and such. Them must of been tradin' post Indians, because they ain't left a two-bit piece in the whole damned bunch, far as I can find out."

"They were soldiers. They probably didn't have two bits. Get back on your horse."

Calvin showed some disposition to argue, then shrugged it off. "Wasn't findin' nothin' noway."

David read the letter through. His first reaction was surprise. He had taken it for granted that this was a Union detail out simply to harass straggling Confederates. It was more than that. The letter, addressed to Captain Tad Smith, was an order for Smith to take a detail to the Owen Townsend ranch west of the Pecos River. There he was to prepare

for immediate shipment a store of rifles, ammunition and
powder which had been cached by Union troops as they
fled northward the year before. They had not wanted it falling into Confederate hands but had not wished to destroy
it, either. Now, the letter said, they had use for it in the
pursuit and chastisement of the Texan invaders.

> A train of ten wagons will be dispatched from
> this point on the 10th instant, and should reach
> the Townsend rancho within two days after your
> arrival. Townsend and his household have already
> left here and should be returned to their place of
> residence before you reach it.
>
> They are loyal to the Union; therefore you will
> render all possible service and show utmost cour-
> tesy. Townsend was a valued scout for General
> Kearney's incursion into the Territory fifteen years
> ago, and the family has been of material aid to us
> in the current difficulties. You may place fullest
> reliance in the word and advice of my friend Owen
> Townsend.
>
> I need not remind you how badly this cache of
> munitions is needed for the continuation of our
> successful campaign to push the rebellious Texans
> from our borders and to pursue them into their
> own lair.
>
> Benj. Stahl,
>
> Colonel, Commanding

David looked around him at the dead men. They would
never finish that mission now, or any other. When those
wagon people got to the cache, they would probably wonder why the escort never showed up.

The young trooper Richey rode up to David. He was visi-
bly shaking. His eyes apprehensively searched the rocky
sides of the pass. "We done picked up everything we think
would be of any use, Lieutenant. We've found some tinned

rations, a few canteens and such. If you're waitin' on us, there ain't no use you wastin' any more of your time."

David nodded. "Nothin' is keepin' us here."

Richey glanced at one of the bodies and turned his face quickly away. "We goin' to leave them layin' here thisaway?"

"You want us to take time to bury them?"

"Anywhere else it would seem like the Christian thing. But this ain't no Christian place."

"No, it sure isn't." David made a signal and led the men out of the pass, heading south. Hernandez came down from his post on the west rim and looked at David. David signaled for him to go ahead and take the point. Hernandez hunched a little and went on. Sergeant Mitchell rode off of the east rim and fell in beside David as they proceeded in a stiff trot, putting the pass as far behind them as they could without overtaxing the horses.

Mitchell said, "I spotted a packmule out yonder a ways. He must've stampeded out of the pass, and the Indians either didn't catch him or forgot about him."

"We'll pick him up." David was only half listening. His mind dwelt on those Yankees back there. He still held the letter in his hand, crumpled. He unfolded it and glanced over it again. Gradually he realized something that he had passed over lightly the first time: a detail of wagons was on its way to collect the cache. Unless good fortune should strike twice and the Indians should eliminate the wagon train too, the mission probably would still be accomplished, even without the captain and his men.

David reflected on the potential destructive power in ten wagons of munitions. If those Yankees recovered the cache they would use it to guarantee that some Texans never saw home again.

Sergeant Mitchell was talking, but David only nodded, agreeing to comments he didn't really hear. He noticed some lines on the back of the letter. They were a crude map, directions for finding the Townsend place. They were probably enough for someone who knew this part of the country, but to David they were a little vague.

His pulse began to beat with an excitement different from the kind he had felt facing those Indians. He looked up, his eyes widening. Sergeant Mitchell continued to talk, and David had not heard a word he said. He studied Mitchell now, still not hearing. He had never been comfortable in the sergeant's presence, but the feeling was of a personal nature, a realization that he was in a position that morally belonged to Mitchell, and some doubt whether he was worthy of it. It had nothing to do with Mitchell's ability as a soldier. If he had nineteen men like Noley Mitchell, he could turn around and give the damnyankees a whipping right here and now, and make them yearn for Colorado and California.

He frowned, wondering what Mitchell would think about the idea that was beginning to build in his mind.

He turned and looked back at the other men. He saw Gene Ivy, gazing worriedly toward the hills where the Indians had disappeared. The lad meant well and could perform if told exactly what to do, but he seemed unable to initiate anything on his own.

Pete Richey. Willing also, but young, green, perhaps of less potential even than Ivy. The two boys, he had been told, had come from neighboring farms, had ridden together to the appointed marshaling place for recruits, had listened to the same patriotic speeches, and had told the same lie about their ages to join.

T. E. Storey, who rode almost sideways now, looking back toward the pass they had left. From what Mitchell had said the day David had been assigned to this unit, Storey had been a town policeman. That, in David's view, should have been a good background for a soldier. But Mitchell had been disparaging. "When they can't make it anywhere else, they become city policemen," the ex-sheriff had said. David was vaguely aware of the traditional rivalry between county and city officials. He tended to regard Mitchell's judgment as colored by prejudice. Storey, David thought, should be a man he could rely on in a pinch.

Aaron Bender, from whom David had not heard a dozen words. Maybe quiet men were the best soldiers. Certainly the loud ones usually were not.

Jake Calvin, David had already decided, was not one to count on in time of trouble. In a couple of skirmishes with

Union details Calvin had hung back, staying low and out of the line of fire as much as he could. He became fierce after the battle, but only in his talk.

He was still in doubt about Homer Gilman, a miller by trade, a tall, gaunt man who had little to say but always stuck close by Noley Mitchell. He was very plainly a Mitchell partisan.

There were Patrick O'Shea and Otto Hufstedler, an unlikely pair to be close friends. O'Shea was fairly freshly arrived from the old sod. Hufstedler had come to Texas with a tide of German immigrants in the 1850s, the young men like himself trying to avoid conscription into a German Army they hated. Now he found himself in an army anyway, a volunteer fighting for a cause he probably did not understand, struggling with a language still difficult for him. He and O'Shea seemed always to be together. The only common bond David could see was that both were immigrants. Perhaps that was it, that they felt shut out to some degree from other company. That was a feeling David understood very well.

Fermin Hernandez. Accounts indicated he had been an oxcart freighter on the road between San Antonio and the Rio Grande by way of rowdy Helena and points south, no place for a weak or timid man. It was said that Hernandez had done some smuggling when it came handy. That was against the law but was hardly considered a moral offense in that time and place; everybody beyond the age of seven did some of it. They saw no way a government could be harmed by a bit of trading between people of two neighboring countries and regarded the customs laws as principally designed to provide wages to lazy government employees who should have been lending their minds and muscle to honest endeavor. Hernandez never volunteered to talk about himself, and David hadn't asked. A Mexican's affairs were his own business so long as they did not encroach on those of the Anglo. That was the code of the times.

Luther Lusk. David's face pinched as he gazed at the man. From fragments he had heard, he gathered that Lusk had had some disagreements with the law back home, represented by Noley Mitchell, but that they had come together willingly against a common enemy. It was said they had been enemies once, but here they were friends, and David had sensed a bond of sorts between them, a respect that honest enemies sometimes develop for one another. Exactly what Lusk had done for a living was unclear. David had heard or seen indications that he had had some experience at freighting, as had Hernandez, and at scouting on the Indian frontier for the Ranger service. If the latter were true, David doubted that it had lasted long. Lusk showed little inclination to follow orders from anybody, and the Rangers were a quasi-military organization. They could not have depended upon a man of such independent mind for very long, David reasoned. Certainly he knew that *he* could not depend upon him.

The other men were of varied stripe and hue. David had not come to know them much in his limited time with the outfit. They were still little more than names to him, names and faces but not personalities. They showed little interest in becoming anything more, at least for him.

Sergeant Mitchell stood in his stirrups periodically and searched the hills with his eyes. He took off his threadbare remnant of a gray coat, for the sun was beginning to warm him. He rubbed a shirtsleeve across his sweaty forehead. "How long you figure now to Fort Bliss, Davey?"

David was paying so little attention that Mitchell had to ask him twice. David said, "I don't know." He was still crumpling the letter in his hand. He frowned, glancing back once more at the men behind him.

They could do it. Hell, yes, they could do it, if they put their minds to it and had the will.

"Sergeant, I wish you'd read this and tell me what you think."

Mitchell held the letter out at arm's length, squinting. When he had read it, he turned it over and examined the map. He traced with his finger and pointed to a spot. "I'd say we're somewhere along here, wouldn't you?"

David didn't care to let it be known, but he had more faith in Mitchell's sense of time and position. "I would imagine so."

"And . . ."—Mitchell traced the map on down toward the bottom—"there is the Townsend place. Some east of our present line of travel, wouldn't you say?"

"I'd say so," David agreed, leaning again on Mitchell's judgment.

"I believe I know what you're thinkin', Davey."

"That we could stop those munitions from fallin' back into Union hands. That we could keep them from bein' used against Texas."

Mitchell pondered. "Some of these old boys might not like it much, us goin' out of our way. They can already smell Texas in the wind."

"That's why I'd rather not tell them till I have to."

Mitchell's heavy eyebrows knitted. It was clear that he did not relish being a partner in any conspiracy. "They may not take it kindly."

"They haven't taken kindly to anything else I've done. It's a soldier's place to carry out orders, not to ask questions."

"That's when you're winnin'. But when you're losin', a man starts watchin' out for his own hide."

"So we tell them when we have to, and not before."

"You're the officer. I just ain't sure it's totin' fair."

"If we told them, how many would we lose?"

"A few might take and leave us. But they'll have to know sooner or later. You can't fool them all the way."

"Maybe I can fool them to a point that they have no choice."

"They've always got a choice, Davey. Anytime it gets dark, they have a choice."

David glanced back at the men trailing him and felt a moment of quiet envy. All they had to do was follow. They didn't have to take responsibility or make decisions. They didn't have to take the blame for an officer's mistakes, if they could live through them.

Times like this he wished he were back in Texas trading horses and mules, able to fall back on the comfort and security of his father's name.

But it was a long way to Texas.

2

~~~~

If there had been any talk in the men, the bitter day had worn it out of them. They rode in stolid silence through the dry and alien hills. Hernandez was out front as scout, the lieutenant and Mitchell next, riding together. Before sundown they stopped to cook a light supper at a spring they came across, using rations from the pack of the Yankee mule they had picked up along the way.

They brewed their first coffee in many days. Lacking any grinder for the Yankee coffee beans, they put them in a leather pouch and beat them to pieces with a rock.

No man here was acquainted with this region. They filled the canteens, for there might be water again across the next hill, or this might be the last for a hundred miles. The sun's warmth faded quickly in the late afternoon, and by sundown most of the men had their coats on, buttoned against the chill. After a brief supper they rode a few more miles to put the campfires behind them in case Indians or Yankees might smell the smoke. They made a dry, fireless camp in a cover of scrub timber.

No one argued about taking his turn standing guard, and David had little concern about someone falling asleep at it. The memory of those dead Yankees made it difficult to sleep even when off guard duty.

They brewed coffee in the cold light of a mountain dawn and chewed hardtack found on the packmule. By good daylight they were moving southward again, edging gradually eastward. In midafternoon they came across a tiny Mexican settlement, surrounded by a few small fields just starting to get their spring work. Across the valley David saw a scattered band of sheep trying to find the first green picking of spring but crowding the season a little. He had seen dozens of these villages spread across this territory. They were largely self-sufficient, producing almost everything the people needed for their own survival. In the days of Spanish colonialism and later Mexican rule, they had been too far removed to receive much help from the government; virtually the only officials they ever saw were the tax collectors, who always seemed to find them about once a year. The government agents brought nothing but took much away. These villages were only minimally affected by the trade that went on between New Mexico and the northern Mexican states such as Chihuahua. If they couldn't grow it or make it, they did without.

The people were usually wary of strangers. David had found in them little inclination to fraternize with the Confederates. He doubted that they had been warmer to the Yankees. They were sufficient unto themselves.

As a precaution he spread the troopers in skirmish-line fashion rather than let them ride into the village in a tight group, an easier target. He signaled Hernandez to wait for him, and the two rode toward the little plaza side by side, suspiciously eyeing the houses and the corrals, looking for any sign that there might be people here beyond the native villagers.

The women and the children who had been outside seemed to melt quietly away, disappearing into the houses. By the time David and Hernandez reached the plaza, only two persons remained in sight, one an old man with a gray, stringy beard, perhaps the village patriarch, and a *padre* standing in the door of the little mud church.

David raised one hand in a sign that he came in peace and reined toward the old man. The *viejo* eyed him with suspicion and a trace of fear. Through long generations, strangers had seldom brought good tidings to these settlements. The old man could clearly tell that these bedraggled *Tejanos* brought nothing with them that would enrich his village. The people would be most fortunate if these foreigners did not bring misfortune of some description; most did.

"Tell him we're friendly," David said to Hernandez. He had been around Texas Mexicans enough to sense that Hernandez was translating faithfully. But the old man's half-whispered reply meant nothing to him, and he could tell even Hernandez had trouble with it. Hernandez had complained before that these New Mexico people spoke a brand of Spanish different from his own. They had been isolated for generations, and their little contact was with a different part of Mexico than that known to the Texas Mexicans. It stood to reason that the dialects were worlds apart.

"He says he is grateful," Hernandez translated. "He asks what we want of him."

"We'll take nothin' from his village and hurt no one. All we want is information."

As Hernandez relayed the message, David saw the old man ease a little, though still wary. Texans had been portrayed to these people as first cousins of the devil, and some had gone to considerable lengths to prove it.

"Ask him if he has seen any Union troops."

The old man assured him that none of the *Americanos* had been seen here in many months, not since the *Tejanos* had driven them north.

David was inclined to believe him, though he could never be certain about these people. They were Mexicans, and as a Texan he would always remember the Alamo. "Ask him how far it is to the ranch of Owen Townsend, and what direction it lays in."

Hernandez glanced at David with surprise. This was the first he had heard of a Townsend ranch. He asked David to repeat the name, then translated the question. For a moment David thought he saw recognition in the watery brown eyes. But when the answer came back through Hernandez, it was to the effect that the *viejo* knew no Owen Townsend.

David frowned. "Ask again. Be sure he understood the name."

The answer was the same. Clearly, Townsend was a *gringo* name. The people in this village rarely saw a *gringo*.

David's instincts told him the man was lying. He was certain he had seen recognition, just for a moment. To know nothing was a form of defense these people had long used to avoid involvement in events which were none of their affair. What they did not know, they could not tell. What they did not tell would bring no reprisal.

Hernandez shrugged. "He lies, I think. But if he don't want to tell, he don't. Who is this Townsend? What for do you ask of him?"

"*I'll* ask the questions."

Hernandez ignored David's reply. "Is it for this Townsend that we go always a bit to the east, instead of only to the south? To get to Paso del Norte we should be closer to the Rio Grande, but we move toward the Pecos. Since yesterday I have wanted to ask you about this."

"I have my reasons. You will not talk of this to the other men."

Hernandez made no attempt to hide his suspicion. He gave David no response, neither promise nor denial. David knew that in all likelihood every man would know as soon as they stopped for supper.

He looked again at the old Mexican and resisted a moment of violent temptation. If the patriarch did not choose to speak, he would not, and that was the end of it.

As always, they rode until an hour before dark, then stopped to fix a hot supper over tiny fires they hoped would make little smoke and be unseen. During this time he noticed several of the men in conversation with Hernandez and glancing in the lieutenant's direction. Eight or ten of them converged on David. Luther Lusk was in the lead, bristling.

"Buckalew, who's this Towser you was askin' about?"

David gave Hernandez a hard look. "Townsend," he corrected.

"Why are you askin' about him? What business have we got anywhere besides Fort Bliss and Paso del Norte?"

David saw that the rest of the men were watching curiously from afar. He was reluctant to give it all away because he didn't trust their reaction. He stared at the fire a little and then asked, "Are you proud of the way we're goin' home, Lusk, chastised by the Yankees?"

"You know I ain't. None of us are."

"What if we were given one last chance to hit them a lick—not a flea bite but a hard lick that would really hurt them?"

Lusk frowned at Sergeant Mitchell, then looked back at David. "Have you talked it over with Noley?"

"It's not his decision to make; it's mine."

Lusk's frown deepened, along with his suspicions. "If Noley don't like it, I don't."

Heat began rising in David's blood. He repeated what he had said, about it being his decision, not Mitchell's. Lusk ignored him and looked to the sergeant.

Mitchell had listened quietly, sipping his coffee. Reluctantly he said, "You'd better tell them, Davey."

David didn't think so, but he felt himself hemmed in.

Lusk continued to push. "If it's a decent idea you'll tell us about it. Let us decide what *we* think."

Resentment fired David's face. This was not the way a military unit was supposed to operate. The more time the men had to think about it, the more arguments they might raise against it. But he bowed to the inevitable. "All right, since everybody wants so damned bad to know, I'll tell you." He waved for all the men to gather around, including those still fixing their suppers.

One lesson old officers had drilled into him was that to keep control of the men you always start out on the offensive and never take a defensive tack with them. "By rights," he declared sternly, "I ought not to tell you a thing, and you ought not to ask. It's a soldier's job to follow orders and ask no questions." He saw that the lecture was lost on these men. They were soldiers only by their own consent, and that consent had been but tentatively given. They had responded patriotically and on impulse to a call that their country needed them. That need, in their view, had involved whipping hell out of the Yankees, not relinquishing their individuality and manhood.

David took the letter from his pocket and read it aloud, allowing time for its import to soak in on the men. He remembered that it had taken a while before he had seen its potential. "So there it is, ten wagons of arms and powder. All that, lyin' there waitin' for them to use against us. We're the only Texans who know about it. It's up to us to blow it to Kingdom Come."

Trooper T. E. Storey looked at Luther Lusk, as if assessing his possible support. "What if there's already Yankees there, guardin' it?"

David said, "That bunch of Yankees the Indians killed . . . they were bein' sent to do that and to wait for the wagons. There's no reason to expect anybody to be there except the ranch people."

"And how many of *them* is there likely to be? I've known of ranch people in Texas that stood off a hundred Comanches, just maybe three or four of them, forted up good. How many would it take to stand off the twenty of us?"

David challenged, "How many of us stand likely to be killed if the Yankees get ahold of all that ammunition?"

"None, if we move fast enough and beat them back to Texas."

Stiffly David said, "We came out here to do a job for our country. As it stands right now, we got our butts kicked. When we signed up in San Antonio we took a pledge to do the best that was in us. Well, I think there's still better in us than we've shown. Till we've done this job or busted a gut tryin', how can we say we've done our best? We won't be able to look people in the face and say we've tried."

Storey was not converted. "Who we goin' to look in the face if we're dead? What if we decide not to go?"

David's eyes narrowed. "You'll go. I'll lead you if I can. If I can't, I'll drive you."

Storey stared at him in sullen silence.

Luther Lusk turned to Noley Mitchell. "It's up to you, Noley. What do you say?"

At that moment David resented Noley Mitchell, but he tried not to show it.

Mitchell didn't hesitate. "I think we ought to go and do it."

Lusk nodded. "That's good enough for me. If you say so, Noley, we'll follow you."

Follow the sergeant, not the lieutenant. David gritted his teeth. "We can make some more distance before dark." Most of them hadn't finished supper yet, but he motioned for Hernandez to lead out and pointed the direction, south-east. They rode into the darkness.

Mitchell kept his horse beside David a long time before he volunteered, "Davey, I know you and the men have got off on the wrong foot with each other. But they're a good bunch, mostly. You got to have patience and trust them more."

David didn't reply.

They made a quiet, dry camp, the night chill biting to the bone as David wrapped his one woolen blanket around him and stretched on the ground. He slept fitfully, the arm bothering him a lot. Dreams came to him in patches and fragments. The pain took him back to the army hospital in Albuquerque. For a time he dimly saw a woman bent over him, wrapping the wound with gentle hands, trying not to hurt him. He tried to see her face, but it never came clear. It never had.

He awoke to the realization that someone was shaking his arm, bringing on a stabbing pain. Noley Mitchell was kneeling beside him, the first pink light of dawn reflected in his grim face. "Davey, we've got two men gone."

Casting off the blanket, David moved quickly to his feet, looking around him in the semidarkness He hoped one of them was Luther Lusk.

Mitchell said, "That's the way with them city policemen. It was T. E. Storey and Aaron Bender. They must of left durin' Storey's watch."

Two men! David clenched his fists in frustration. The odds had been long enough when they were twenty. Now they were eighteen.

Mitchell scowled. "I ain't told you the worst of it yet. They taken some of our rations with them. We've got little enough as it is. You want me to detail a patrol and trail them?"

David wanted to trail them. He wanted to catch them and perhaps shoot them as an example. He gave way to a string of profanity such as a horse trader is likely to pick up in the course of that uncertain career. It served as a release for the anger and allowed him to regain his balance. Time they spent in pursuit of Storey and Bender would be time lost from the more important job at hand, and perhaps time given to whatever Union troops might be coming along behind them.

"The hell with them. Let's get the men up and move out."

Through the day the men kept quartering eastward, watchfully crossing canyon after canyon, ravine after dry ravine that snaked out in search of the alkaline waters of the Pecos River. Late in the day they came to the turbulent brown stream that etched its way between the mountains and the dreaded plains, the uncharted Llano Estacado. Noley Mitchell went to the edge, filled a canteen and tipped it up to taste of it. He spat most of it out and rubbed a sleeve across his mouth. "Anybody doubts that's the Pecos, just let him drink a little of it. I remember how it tasted when we crossed it before, on the way west."

"That was a long way south of here," David reminded him.

"Distance don't improve it."

Soon afterward, following the river, they came in sight of a Mexican herder tending a large band of Merino sheep. David spurred his horse to catch up to Hernandez, and together they rode to the sheep. He took the herder to be in his mid-twenties. With the country at war, it struck him odd that a man of that prime age should not be serving in the Army—either Union or Confederate—instead of herding sheep out here in a desolate land that to David was little more than desert. These people, so remote from the heavily settled sections, knew little or nothing of the bloody wars fought by civilized men. They were backward in many ways.

The young herder studied the troopers intently, and it occurred to David that among other things he was counting them.

"Ask him about the Townsend ranch," David said to Hernandez.

To his surprise an answer was freely given, without the hesitation he had seen in the old man in the last village. Hernandez turned. "He says he has heard of it but he was never there himself, so he cannot tell just where it is. But he says there is a trading post south of here where we can ask, and he thinks those people will tell us. He says there is food to buy in the post, and much whisky."

"Last thing we need right now is whisky," David said darkly, looking toward the men behind him. He had never been with them in a place where they had been tested by whisky; he had no idea who or how many might give him a problem. "Ask him if he has seen any Yankees."

Hernandez relayed the question, then turned with a quizzical expression. "He asks, what is a Yankee?"

Backward! David thought again. How could these people exist way out here, cut off from all that was important in the world?

Later the Texans stopped for supper, then made their customary ride into the first hour of darkness. David quietly studied each man, looking for signs that would tell him who might be contemplating desertion tonight, following the example of Storey and Bender. David slept a little early in the night, but the worry over desertions brought him fully awake with every changing of the guard, and during the last two shifts he slept none at all. He sat up with the blanket pulled around his shoulders. He shivered from the chill and counted the sleeping men time and time again, looking sharply every time one turned or groaned in his sleep. At daylight he still had seventeen men.

The one cup of hot coffee failed to take the chill out of his bones. Riding along, he kept glancing at the rising sun, wishing it carried more warmth. By now, down in his part of Texas, the nights would be passable, and the days would even be getting a little hot. There would be a good green tinge in the grass, and the brush would be putting on leaves. Here, farther north and at a higher altitude, it was still more winter than spring.

He could not help wondering, at such a time, what he was doing so far from Texas.

At midmorning Hernandez topped over a rise and reined up suddenly. He turned and looked back, his eyes searching out David. He did not have to signal; his manner was enough. David spurred up to him.

Hernandez pointed. "The trading post, Lieutenant."

It lay a quarter mile down the slope, just far enough from the river to be out of the flood plain. David took out the spyglass. He looked first for any sign of Yankee troops. He saw a scattering of horses and a fair number of mules, mostly of the Spanish type he had seen all over New Mexico. He saw few he thought were of Army caliber.

It wasn't much of a settlement, even by the standards of this sparsely settled country. He saw one long L-shaped adobe building and a squat storehouse behind it. Beyond that was a brush corral where some of the Spanish-looking ponies stood listlessly as if waiting for somebody to fetch them a handful of hay, and doubting that anybody would. Scattered all about was the litter of filth accumulated during years of careless living.

A sleepy-looking place, an unlikely place for trouble. Yet it gave him a feeling of uneasiness that earlier villages had not.

It came to him that he saw no women or children out stirring, as would usually be the case. It struck him that this place looked different from the family villages he had seen so much; it lacked the scattering of adobe and brush houses.

Hernandez seemed to share David's misgivings. "You know what I think, Lieutenant?"

"I'd like to hear it."

"You have heard of the Comancheros?"

The word was dimly familiar. That it had to do with Comanches was obvious, but he could not remember the connection. He had never moved in real Indian country, and he knew only what he had retained from things he had been told.

"I have heard talk of them up here," Hernandez said. "They are people—Mexicans mostly—who go out on the *llano* and do trade with the Indians. The Comanches and Kiowas and whatever others there are, they steal far south in Texas, and down in Mexico. They bring here what they have taken, or near here, out on the plains. The Comancheros trade them what they want—blankets and guns and whisky. They get horses and cattle from the Indians . . . sometimes even women and children slaves the Indians have stolen. That is what the people in the villages have told me. This is a very old thing, a very old trade. Maybe so these are Comancheros. It could be a very bad place."

Noley Mitchell had ridden up and heard most of it. David looked at him, asking a question with his eyes that rank made it awkward to ask in words. Mitchell said, "I've heard of them too, Davey. He could be right. Smart thing would be to go around."

David considered that. "But we might go around the Townsend place too and never know it. We'll ride in there and ask, just Hernandez and me. You'll stay here with the rest of the men."

"You may wish you had us."

"Give us ten minutes, then spread out wide and come in closer to the village. But don't come all the way in unless you see or hear signs of trouble. If that happens, come runnin'."

Mitchell clearly had reservations, but he nodded. "However you want it, Davey."

David thought of the spyglass. He handed it to Mitchell and moved forward. He and Hernandez rode side by side, two tired, dusty men who had little in common except the country they came from. David Buckalew was dressed in the leavings of a smart gray uniform, designed by no pattern other than his mother's imagination, because the Confederacy was new and had not settled upon a common style; every officer outfitted himself according to his own fancies, and what was available. Fermin Hernandez, a private soldier, had not even that much outward appearance to tie him to the military, for he had ridden to war in what had been his Sunday mass suit, of black homespun wool. It had been hell through the summer campaign, and by winter, when he really needed it, the fabric had been patched and repatched and worn so thin that it hardly turned back the sharp, cold wind. But Hernandez rode like a soldier, his back straight, his chin out, his eyes alert.

The people at the post would quickly recognize them for what they were, soldiers of the Confederate States of America . . . more specifically, Texas. People in this part of the country had gotten so in the last few months that they knew a Texan as far as they could see him.

David's suspicion about the adobe post did not diminish as he approached it; if anything, his uneasiness grew. His eyes shifted from the building to outlying corrals, to every clump of brush and every pile of trash that might hide a man. Ahead of him he saw two men come out of the long adobe's front door and stand beside it together, waiting. Other men, six in all, scattered on either side, watching the two riders come in. David took most of them to be Mexicans, but as he neared he could see that two, at least, were Indians.

He assumed the two in the middle to be in charge. He gave his major attention to these, though none of the others made a move that he did not see. He doubted that anything was getting past Hernandez either, for the Mexican was as tense as a trigger spring.

David tugged gently on the reins and halted the brown horse about three paces in front of the men. He raised his hand with the palm outward, signaling peace, though he had reservations about it. The hard way these men looked at him said little of peace but much of war. His first thought was that they were probably all Yankee sympathizers. On reflection he doubted that. Indians had shown no inclination toward politics; they killed either side with equal fervor.

He stared at the two men immediately in front of him. Because of the portly middle and the liberal sprinkling of gray strands in the man's otherwise black hair, David assumed him to be the *majordomo*. "Tell him we have come here in peace to ask only for information."

Hernandez translated and got back a standard salutation. "He says we are all friends here, that his house is our house."

"I wouldn't have it if he gave it to me," David said. "The whole lot of them would as soon cut our throats as look at us. Tell him I'm pleased at his gracious reception, and that we want to ask directions."

Hernandez started the translation. The man who stood next to the older one took a step forward and said in plain English, "Friend, there is no need for you to work through an interpreter."

David was at first startled, then a little chagrined because this man had understood everything he had said. He still looked like a cutthroat, even if he did speak English.

"You're Texans," the man said. "You're a long way from home."

"But tryin' to get there as quick as we can," David said.

"Seems to me you've lost your way, moving this far east. This can be a poor country for a man who loses his way."

A poor country all around, David thought. He refrained from saying it aloud; he figured he had already said enough of a provocative nature. These people looked as if they might want something to be provoked about. The longer he studied the faces, the less he wanted to prolong the stay.

The man who spoke English was burned dark by the sun, and David had assumed him to be Mexican. Now that he looked closer he saw that the eyes were gray rather than brown, and the features were different from those of most people he had seen here. "You're not Mexican. What are you?"

"I am not anything except simply myself," came the easy answer. "I am Floyd Bearfield."

"Where do you come from?"

"That doesn't matter. What matters is where I am, and I am here. I have been here—or hereabout—for a long time."

An exile, David sensed. Usually a man becomes an exile for something he has done. "These aren't your people."

"They are my people now. I have chosen them and they have accepted me. Probably you are a Texan by accident of birth; you just happened to be born there. I am here because I have *chosen* to be."

Damned poor choice, David thought. But each man to his own taste. "Have you seen any Yankee soldiers?"

"None," said Bearfield. "There is little here to interest soldiers of any kind . . . Union or Southern. We have our own community, our own commerce. We do not need a great deal from the outside, and certainly the outside has little business with us. We do not see many people."

David stared at one of the Indians. He knew little of them, but he assumed this one to be Comanche. He found something incongruous in the coat the man was wearing. It was a white man's. He even imagined he saw something familiar in the coat but knew that could not be so.

David said, "We are lookin' for a certain place. We hoped you could tell us how to find it."

"Perhaps. But you do not want to travel any more today. Get down and we will see what we can find for you to eat, and to drink."

"We haven't the time."

"We might even find other pleasures for you."

"We have to go."

Bearfield was letting his displeasure start to show. "Look to your horses, man. Two good horses, by the look of them, and almost ridden down. They need rest and feed. Get down, and we'll see to it."

The man reached out suddenly and took David's bridle reins. As if by signal, an Indian quickly grabbed the reins of Hernandez' horse. Hernandez looked at David in alarm but made no move, waiting for a sign.

The other men moved in closer. David read the intention in their faces. They were about to pick up two Texas horses, cheap.

Hernandez' hand dipped and came up with a knife from his belt. An Indian dropped a blanket from his shoulders, revealing a hidden rifle. He pointed it at Hernandez.

David stiffened. "Easy, Hernandez. They'll kill you."

"We might," Bearfield nodded, pleased. It had been an easy catch. "Step down easily. Give no one cause to do you violence."

David swallowed. He was not totally surprised at the treachery, but he didn't know what to do about it other than to stall for time. Ten minutes, he had told Mitchell.

"I am an officer of the Confederate Army," he said imperiously. "You will turn my horse loose."

Bearfield shook his head incredulously. "I've found you *Tejanos* to be a thick-headed lot. There *is* no Confederate Army, not out here. You've been slashed and shot and beaten to pieces. Do you think the long arm of Jefferson Davis will reach all the way to the Pecos River because of *you*?" He spat on the dry, powdered ground. "Don't try our patience, Texas. We'll let you walk home if you'll not provoke us. Otherwise we'll drag your bodies down to the river and let *it* carry you back."

David felt cold as he looked into the hard faces. The men had formed a semicircle, trapping him and Hernandez. He looked at the rifles that had materialized, and the knives. It struck him as improbable that these men would let them walk away from here. He made no move to dismount.

Tightly he said, "You're mistaken about the Confederate Army. There *is* one, and part of it is very near. Draw our blood and they'll level this place, and you with it."

Bearfield smiled coldly. "We'll accept that risk. Do you get down, or do we *cut* you down?"

Time for stalling had about run out.

David heard running horses. He saw surprise strike the men on the ground. Some stepped back, confused, fearful.

Mitchell had rushed his ten minutes.

Bearfield turned loose of the reins. Only then did David risk glancing around. Mitchell had deployed the troops in a broad line. They came in with rifles up and ready, trapping Bearfield and his men in the open.

David took his first good breath. Hernandez sighed in relief, still holding the knife. He jabbed the point of it at the hand of the Indian who held his bridle rein. The Indian turned loose, quickly raising the hand to his mouth to suck at the bleeding wound.

David looked at Bearfield again. Grimly he asked, "Was there anything else you wanted to say?"

Bearfield didn't look at him. Sullenly he watched the soldiers come in close. Some of the men around him raised their hands in response to the rifles pointed at them, but Bearfield stood with arms at his side. The portly *majordomo* said something angry to him. Bearfield did not reply.

Noley Mitchell rode up beside David. David said, "Thank you, Sergeant. Your watch must be runnin' fast."

"I watched you through the glass, Davey. Looked like you might be glad to see us."

Luther Lusk reined up by Fermin Hernandez. "You all right, *chili*?" Hernandez assured him he was. Lusk looked accusingly at David. "Noley told you it was risky to come in

here, Buckalew. We could've lost ourselves a good interpreter."

David smarted under the reproach but did not intend to
lose dignity by arguing reasons. He said to Hernandez,
"Call for everybody in the buildin' to come out, or we'll
shoot these men."

Three more Indian men and two Mexicans came from inside. Two slatternly women followed, and finally a young
Mexican girl. All the women were frightened, the girl most
frightened of them all. Her face was bruised and swollen.
Her clothing was ragged, barely enough left of it to cover
her.

"Ask if that's all of them," David said sternly. "Tell them
we'll search the place. If we find anybody hidin', we'll shoot
him. And we'll shoot anybody who runs."

Hernandez relayed the message. The response from the
people in the yard was that all were here.

"All right, men," David said stiffly, "pair up and make a
search. If you find any people, do what I said. Shoot them."
The last part of the order was made in anger. It was quickly
regretted but not withdrawn. Mitchell left four men outside
to stand guard. In a few minutes the soldiers came out.
They found no people hiding in the long building, though
out in back they discovered an old man working in a crude
blacksmith shop and fetched him around.

Young Pete Richey said, "You don't really want us to shoot
him, do you, Lieutenant? He's awful old."

David shook his head, glad the men hadn't taken him
literally. "He's probably deaf . . . didn't hear the order."

The old man asked worried questions in mumbled Spanish; he didn't understand what was going on. He plainly
expected to be killed. He turned to Pete Richey and began
to plead.

Richey grabbed the old man's arm. He grasped the lapel
of the coat the old man was wearing; the coat was much too
big.

"Lieutenant," Richey declared, "I know this coat. It's the
one T. E. Storey was wearin'."

A couple of the other Texans agreed, now that it had been pointed out to them. David saw what appeared to be a blotch of dried blood on the coat. Some attempt had been made to wash it out.

The old man couldn't understand what was being said, but he understood very well the angry tone of the voices. He turned and tried to break away, but his legs faltered. Richey quickly caught him, grabbing a handful of the loose coat.

In panic the old man reached down and picked up a rifle one of the others had dropped on the ground. He whirled. Luther Lusk fired, sending the old man sprawling backward, dead.

It had been so sudden that no one else moved; everybody seemed frozen for a moment. Then Jake Calvin said, "It's plain they killed Storey and Bender. I say we ought to shoot and kill every one of them right where he stands."

David thought Calvin was probably right. His own inclination was to shoot them all, other than the women, on general principles and for the good of the country. But he knew he wouldn't. He glanced at Sergeant Mitchell. "Gather up all the horses and mules into one corral."

Mitchell gave an order and took half a dozen men with him. In a few minutes they were back. The tall Homer Gilman was troubled. "Lieutenant, we found Storey's horse out yonder, and Aaron Bender's."

David and Mitchell gravely exchanged glances. David turned to Bearfield. "Would you like to explain how that came to be?"

Bearfield shrugged defensively. "How would I know? Indians come into this place all the time to trade. You don't ask an Indian where he's been or what he's done. It's nobody's business."

"Which ones came in on those horses?"

Bearfield shrugged again. "I don't know. I wasn't paying attention."

David was fairly sure he could pick out one of them, the one who had worn the coat that had caught his eye as he first rode in here. He knew now: it was Bender's.

He said for all the men to hear, "You see now why we have to stay together. You see what happens to men who go out by themselves."

Jake Calvin's eyes were narrow and angry. "I say we kill them all!"

The Texans' faces showed a majority in the same mood. David remembered his father's account of the difficulty Sam Houston had in preventing his victorious Texan soldiers from killing the captured Mexican general Santa Anna. "I'm tempted like all of you, but we can't be sure they were all in on it." His gaze shifted to Bearfield. "We came here to ask for directions."

"Ask. I'll tell you whatever I know."

"I feel sure you will, because we're takin' you with us."

Bearfield's mouth dropped open. "You'll kill me."

"If we have to. It's up to you to be sure we don't have to."

Bearfield looked quickly at his friends, anxiously seeking help. Evidently none understood what was said. "Where is it you want to go? I'll tell you right here."

"And maybe beat us there, and take a lot of friends with you? You'll come with us, and you'll tell us when I get ready to ask you. You'll stay with us till we get there, so that if you lie to us we can cut your throat." David turned to Mitchell. "Sergeant, take a couple of men and catch out a few of the best horses. We'll need one for Bearfield, and we ought to take four or five more to spare."

Mitchell nodded. "We'll run off the rest, then."

"No. These people could soon catch them. If they try to follow after us they'll have to do it afoot. Shoot everything we don't take."

Bearfield protested, "You wouldn't do that!"

"I'd do worse, if I could. I'd burn this place like some kind of a pesthouse." He knew the adobe building wouldn't catch fire, except perhaps its roof. Even if it did, the smoke might draw unwanted attention.

Mitchell took four men to the corrals. They carried some of the guns the trading-post people had dropped. In a few minutes the firing started. The trading-post men hadn't understood the order, but they understood the shooting, the screaming of horses and mules. They shouted their protests in vain. Bearfield watched in bitter silence.

Presently Mitchell and the men came back leading five horses, one saddled for Bearfield. David noted with satisfaction that the stirrups were taken up close, evidently for a short man. Bearfield was going to ride very uncomfortably.

Mitchell said, "We smashed the rifles. We figured that's what you'd want us to do."

David hadn't thought of it, but he said, "That's fine, Sergeant." He had the men take what they wanted of the weapons lying on the ground, then smash the rest. He told Bearfield to get onto the horse. Bearfield stood sullenly until Mitchell prodded him with a rifle. Mitchell took a short piece of rawhide he had picked up somewhere and tied Bearfield's hands to the big horn of the Mexican saddle.

When the troopers had mounted, David gave Fermin Hernandez a signal to lead off. They began stringing out, most looking back. They would have preferred to leave this post razed, the men all dead.

The Mexican girl shouted and came running after them. David saw one of the trading-post men grab at her, but she eluded him. She came on, running like a frightened rabbit, crying out in excited Spanish. David intended to keep riding, but Hernandez heard her and turned back. David halted reluctantly.

The girl grabbed David's leg and pleaded. Hernandez listened, his face darkening. He said, "The Indians, Lieutenant, they stole her out of Mexico. They sold her to the Comancheros, who have kept her here, prisoner." Eyes narrowed in hatred, he looked back at the post. "They do much bad to her. If she stays, they do bad to her some more."

David was about to explain that they couldn't take care of a woman.

One or more of the trading-post men had gone inside and fetched out hidden rifles. A shot was fired, possibly at David. The girl gasped as the bullet smashed into her back. She rolled forward against David's horse, then collapsed. The brown horse danced excitedly, trying to step away from her. David started to swing down but caught himself. One glance told him she had died instantly.

A cry of rage tore from Hernandez' throat. He brought up his own rifle and fired a quick shot at the crowd at the post. A man pitched forward. With a shout, Hernandez spurred back toward the building. In an instant, half the Texans were beside him, shouting in blood anger, firing as they rode.

David shouted vainly for them to stop. Of those who had hesitated, almost all rode back as a second wave, sweeping across the open ground, cutting off the trading-post men before they had time to reach the safety of the adobe building.

Floyd Bearfield thought it was his chance. He started tugging against the rawhide that bound his hands to the horn. David shoved the muzzle of his pistol against Bearfield's ear. "Try and I'll kill you!"

Only Noley Mitchell and Jake Calvin had held back with David. The rest had charged in, shouting, shooting.

Calvin held his ground, his face twisted. "I hope they don't kill them all. I hope they save one for me."

The shooting was over in a minute. The men came drifting back in threes and fours. They gathered around David and the sergeant in a rough circle, their faces still flushed with the outrage which had driven them. Fermin Hernandez dismounted and knelt silently by the girl. He looked up furiously at Bearfield.

Bearfield saw murder in the Mexican's face. He drew closer to David. "I'm your prisoner. You're not going to let him . . ."

David held his hand toward Hernandez, palm outward. "We need him."

Hernandez seemed strongly moved to do it anyway. But he stopped.

Luther Lusk was one of the last to ride up. He was holding someone in the saddle. "Noley," he called, "we got trouble."

The men pulled quickly aside. Pete Richey was slumped over, blood spreading down across his saddle and over his horse's shoulder. Gene Ivy and Homer Gilman, on the ground, got hold of him and eased him down. Lusk dismounted quickly and knelt by the boy. "Step back a little.

Let me see to him." He ripped the coat and shirt away. The wound was in the left shoulder. The bullet had gone all the way through.

Gene Ivy cried out at the sight. He and Richey had grown up together.

Patrick O'Shea said, "I saw whisky in the building. I'll go and fetch it."

David called after him to come back, that he didn't want another man shot there. Luther Lusk said, "Don't worry about him, Buckalew. Ain't nobody alive down there except the women."

In minutes O'Shea was back with a jug. Lusk tipped it up for a long swallow and shook his head violently. "Vile," he gritted. "But it'll clean out a wound."

Richey was still conscious, though the color had drained from his face, leaving it a bluish white. David felt cold, looking at him. The thing had been unnecessary; they shouldn't have charged back on that place. But it was done now. Recriminations wouldn't help anything.

Lusk finished the bandaging. "He oughtn't to ride."

David cursed under his breath. "We can't stay, and we can't leave him here. He's got to ride."

Lusk declared, "We didn't have to come into this post in the first place, Buckalew. Noley tried to tell you we oughtn't to."

David shouldn't have answered, but he couldn't help it. "I didn't order that charge. I tried to stop it." The words were hollow; the thing was done. "Get him onto his horse."

He saw Bearfield staring grimly back toward the post. Everything down there was quiet and still.

David said, "Bearfield, you're as safe as any of us so long as you try no tricks. Behave yourself and we'll turn you loose when we're through. Cross us and we'll leave you layin' like your friends back yonder."

He gave Hernandez a nod. The Mexican took a last look at the girl, her small, fragile body lying smashed on the ground. Then he set out again to point the way south.

3

They rode a long time in moody silence. David did not want to set new directions too quickly lest their destination be anticipated by anyone following behind them. Late in the afternoon they made their usual stop to fix supper. Over a steaming cup of coffee, David stared coldly at Bearfield. The trader kept his gaze on the ground, but a gnawing anxiety showed in his face.

"Hernandez says you're a Comanchero. It strikes me that you're probably a man with a lot of blood on your hands."

"I never liked that word 'Comanchero.' But Comancheros are simply traders. That's all *I* am. I buy and sell. I never kill anybody, Buckalew."

"But you make a market for those that do. You buy bloodstained goods. That makes you part of the killin'."

"I don't kill people."

"You were about to kill me and Hernandez." He decided the exchange was a waste of time. He asked, "Do you know Owen Townsend?"

He saw instant recognition in Bearfield's eyes, and perhaps even more than that. But Bearfield chose not to acknowledge it. "Townsend? What does he do?"

"He has a place somewhere. Either you know him or you don't. If you don't, you're of no use to us. The guarantee is off."

"I know him," Bearfield admitted grudgingly. His dislike was evident.

David's father had taught him that a man should be judged by his enemies as well as by his friends. Bearfield's enmity spoke favorably for Owen Townsend, Yankee or not. David said, "You're takin' us to his place."

Bearfield looked sharply at him. "Me, to Townsend's place? You don't know what you're asking. Anyway, I can't imagine what he has that you would want. If I know Townsend he's no friend of yours. He probably raises the Union flag in his bedroom."

"All you have to do is take us there."

Bearfield plainly disliked the prospect. "I would go around his place if I were you. He has nothing you need."

"Eat your supper. We'll move on in a few minutes."

The look of anxiety clung to Bearfield. "Even if he doesn't try to kill you, he'll probably try to kill *me*."

"What have you done to him?"

Bearfield's jaw tightened. He didn't answer.

David didn't care whether Bearfield ate supper or not. He was considerably more concerned about Pete Richey. The boy had been stretched out to rest on a blanket. Luther Lusk squatted beside him, chewing hardtack and sipping coffee, his eyes on the boy. David studied Lusk in silence. In the time he had been with the outfit he had not seen one thing in Lusk that he liked, one thing to give him any idea that Lusk was capable of concern over anyone except himself. But now he hovered over Pete Richey like some mother hen.

Richey lay still, his eyes closed. David couldn't tell whether he was conscious or not. "Has he eaten anything?"

Lusk grunted. "Did you think he would?"

"I hoped he might. He'll need his strength."

"How's he goin' to have any strength? He's been losin' blood, and he'll keep losin' it if he has to ride again."

"We can't stay here. We might *all* lose blood."

Lusk's eyes showed he was spoiling for a fight. "If there's anybody comin', this is as good a place as any. We can whip them here."

David said dubiously, "I never noticed you take an interest in this boy before."

"He never was hurt before." Lusk clenched his fist and cast a threatening look at Floyd Bearfield. "I've known his old daddy down home for a long time. He done me a favor once. A lifesavin' favor, you could call it."

David said, without conviction, "We'll get his boy back to him."

Lusk scowled. "I wisht I thought so."

Noley Mitchell eased over close, asking with his eyes if David needed help. David shook his head and walked away. "Finish up," he said loudly to everybody. "We'll travel a ways before dark." He could feel Lusk's hard eyes on his back; he didn't have to look. He motioned for trooper Homer Gilman to tie Bearfield's hands to the saddlehorn again. Gene Ivy was closer, but David wasn't certain of the youth's competence; he didn't want Bearfield taking advantage and getting away.

Bearfield said resentfully, "I won't run off."

"You bet you won't. Now, which way do we go from here?"

Bearfield cursed under his breath but did not otherwise resist. "Down the river. He built close to the water. There isn't enough water in this country that a man can locate just anywhere he wants to."

As he rode, David watched Bearfield. He began to notice that Bearfield sat straight in the saddle, with the style of a military man. He regarded the thought as an unlikely one. Why would a military man be living in the middle of nowhere with a set of cutthroats and thieves? But the notion kept nagging at him. Finally he asked.

Bearfield replied with bitterness. "Do I look like a soldier?"

"As a matter of fact, you do."

The wind was out of the south, and presently it brought David the faint smell of smoke. He saw that Mitchell had caught it too. "Not a grass fire, Davey," Mitchell said. "We'd see the sign of it, I think. This smells more like wood."

David turned in the saddle. "Bearfield, how far to Townsend's?"

Bearfield looked him in the eye without wavering. "Not far."

"Close enough to smell the smoke of their fires?"

"Perhaps."

David tried to read something in Bearfield's face, but the man had the air of a card player, his eyes a mask. Hernandez was about fifty yards out in front, moving up a steep rise in the fading red light of the afternoon sun. David was on the point of sending someone up to tell him to stop. Suddenly Hernandez halted at the top of the hill, turning his horse quickly and coming down. He was frantically signaling for the troops behind him to halt as he spurred back toward them. He pulled up in front of David, his horse's hind feet sliding, raising a little cloud of dust.

"Indians, Lieutenant! A camp of them is there, just over that hill." His face was flushed. He looked back over his shoulder as if he expected pursuit.

David asked urgently, "You think they saw you?"

"I don't know. I see *them,* and that is enough."

For a moment Bearfield was forgotten. He seized the opportunity to drum his heels against his horse's ribs. The horse started south in a run. David dropped his hand toward his rifle, then realized the danger in firing. "Don't anybody shoot!"

Several men spurred after Bearfield. Luther Lusk was in the lead. He caught up and grabbed at Bearfield's reins, at the same time ramming Bearfield's horse. The jolt bounced Bearfield up onto the cantle of his saddle. While he was out of balance Lusk gave him another hard bump, almost knocking the horse off of its feet. Bearfield slipped from the saddle and then began dragging, his hands tied to the horn, the brush tearing at his legs. He cried out from the pain.

Lusk got hold of the reins and took the horse into a wide circle, then brought him back toward David in a smart trot. He let Bearfield drag. He stopped beside David and held out Bearfield's reins as an offering. His voice was cold. "Here, Buckalew. You lost this."

Bearfield tried to pull himself up, tugging against the big horn of the Mexico saddle. The lower legs of his trousers were shredded. Blood showed on the frayed cloth around the knees.

"You lied to us," David accused. "Our deal was no tricks."

"I didn't lie to you," Bearfield said in a subdued voice, pinched with pain. "The Townsend place is down the river."

Maybe it was and maybe it wasn't. "But you didn't tell us about that Indian camp."

"Indians move around. You never know where they'll be."

"I'm bettin' you knew these were here. You figured to lead us into the midst of them and get us all killed, and yourself set free."

Bearfield's chest heaved; the jolting had pounded much of the breath from him. "Are you going to leave me dragging like this?"

David's foot was in the right position to kick Bearfield in the face. The temptation was strong. He turned. "Smith, you have a rope. Put a loop over Bearfield's neck."

Bearfield stared with wide eyes. "You wouldn't hang me."

"I would if I saw a tree big enough. The next time you run, we'll see how far your neck stretches."

David kept glancing at the hill beyond which Hernandez had seen the Indian camp. He could still smell the woodsmoke, drifting on the south wind. He was beginning to feel that the Indians hadn't seen Hernandez. A scouting party would have been here by now.

He considered his options. To cross over the Pecos at this point would be relatively easy, for it was not wide or turbulent here. But it was some distance east to any hills that might hide them from view of the Indian camp. Moreover, he considered it probable they might run into more Indians in that direction, toward the open plains. That possibility would probably be lessened if they moved back toward the New Mexico settlements. He looked at Hernandez and pointed west. "We won't let you get so far out in front from now on. We'll be close behind you if you run into anything."

Hernandez said nothing to indicate any gratitude.

They rode long into the darkness, putting miles between themselves and the Indian camp. For a time David kept Homer Gilman as a rear guard trailing some distance behind them out of concern that Indians might even yet ride in upon them. This concern did not leave him until night. The moon was late in rising, so they rode in almost pitchblackness. As the moon came up, David spotted a dark motte of brush in the silver light. He gave quiet orders for pitching a dry, cold camp. He had Bearfield's hands tied to a

tree. Bearfield complained that he could not sleep that way.
Jake Calvin suggested that he knew how to put him to
sleep. The complaints stopped.

Some of the men were without blankets. Several had volunteered their own in an effort to make Pete Richey as comfortable as they could. The boy was in considerable pain.

At daybreak Bearfield still lay where David had put him,
his hands securely tied. If he had tried anything, half a
dozen men would have fought over the privilege of killing
him, and he knew it. His body was cramped from the uncomfortable positions to which his bonds had limited him.
His eyes were streaked red; he hadn't slept.

Pete Richey lay awake, face pale and twisted with pain.
David said, "You just keep ahold. We'll get there."

He judged that they could cut back toward the river now.
A southeasterly course should bring them in well below the
Indian camp. He hoped it would not bring them in below
the Townsend place as well. Bearfield assured him it would
not, and David had little choice but to gamble along. Perhaps by this time Bearfield was fearful enough of these Texans not to try springing any more traps.

They came back onto the river at midmorning. Bearfield
was looking around with considerable agitation. David had
an uneasy feeling he might know something he wasn't sharing. But presently Bearfield said, "You'll find the ranch just
a short distance now, straight down the river."

"How far?"

"You'll see it soon. When are you going to set me loose?"

"When I get ready."

"I don't want to go all the way in to that ranch."

"We haven't seen it yet, much less gotten there."

Bearfield had told the truth. Hernandez stopped when
his horse topped the next rise. He took a long look and rode
back. "Settlement, Lieutenant."

David motioned to Noley Mitchell. The two of them ac-
companied Hernandez back up the hill. Below them perhaps a quarter mile lay an adobe ranch headquarters up the
slope from the banks of the river, just safely beyond danger
of flood. The buildings were clustered as in a fort, an open
space around them, surrounded by a cedar picket fence four

to five feet tall. The main building was large and in a hollow square with a typical Mexican patio in the center. David studied it a long time through the glass. He saw only one outside door facing in his direction. The outside windows were few and small, just large enough to let in a minimum of sun and fresh air and to give shooting room for riflemen inside in case of an attack.

The outer picket fence was far enough from the buildings that anyone who scaled it would have to face into open fire while running something like thirty to forty yards. Townsend—or whoever had built it—had intended to be well prepared for hostilities. There had been many enemies to worry about fifteen years ago. There probably still were.

He shuddered, thinking about the fearful price his men would pay if forced to attack that fortification by simple frontal assault, against even half their number of determined riflemen. That smacked of suicide and had no place in his plan.

Outside the picket fence but adjacent to it were two small adobe outbuildings and a pair of adobe-wall corrals, built thick to withstand Indian efforts at cutting them or breaking them down. David saw no gates into them except from within the picket-enclosed compound. To his considerable relief he saw only four horses in the pens. Several more grazed at some distance along the river, sharing the short old grass with some long-legged, long-horned cattle of the Mexican type.

He took that as a hopeful indication they would find few people here. At the distance he couldn't tell if the corraled horses might be military. Probably not, or there would be more. He handed the glass to Mitchell.

Mitchell made a long and careful study. "Looks all right."

David signaled for the rest of the troop to move up. "We'll ride down there in double file like we didn't expect trouble, and chances are there won't be any. If there is, spread out and attack while they're still off balance."

Lusk said sarcastically, "You want Pete Richey to attack too?"

David ignored Lusk and said to the whole command, "We're on a military mission. Let's look like soldiers."

He signaled for Hernandez to stay with the others this time, not to ride out in advance. David himself led the two columns down the hill. He carried his rifle across the pommel of the saddle, his right hand around the trigger guard, ready in event of fire. He consciously straightened his back, trying to give the illusion of military bearing if not the reality.

For a moment his mind went home to his father, and back in time to another war in another place. If Joshua Buckalew were here, he wondered, would he handle this differently? Could he?

The Texans' approach was seen. Three men stepped out of the arched doorway that led into the patio. They moved into the sunlight but stayed near enough that they could quickly dart back into the relative safety of the patio. At least one carried a rifle, but he made no belligerent move with it. This gave David stronger hope that there would be no violence here.

One of the men took an extra couple of steps forward as David came within hailing distance. He carried no rifle. One of his arms hung stiffly at his side. He was an Anglo. The other two men, both younger, were Mexican.

David reined up and saluted. The one-armed man stood stiffly, in a manner suggestive of the military. He responded only with a nod. He raised his left hand in the Indian sign of peaceful intentions.

David said, "You'd be Owen Townsend, I suppose?"

The man seemed mildly surprised at the use of his name. "I am. I did not realize I was known in Texas." His sharp eyes searched David's face for something they didn't find.

"I am David Buckalew, Lieutenant, Confederate Army. My compliments to you, sir." For what, he could not have said.

"And mine to you, sir, and to your men."

Again, David would have been hard put to have found much for either side to compliment the other about. The Texans were a hard-used bunch, and this cedar-picket and adobe civilian fort was hardly a thing of classic beauty.

Townsend's voice was civil but not friendly. "Get down. I imagine you're all hungry. There isn't much here, but we always willingly share whatever there is."

"Much obliged, Mister Townsend. Our first need is some medical supplies. We have a wounded man."

Townsend's gaze immediately picked up Pete Richey. "Of course." He turned to one of the Mexicans and spoke in Spanish. The only word David understood was "Martha." That, he assumed, would be Townsend's wife.

Townsend walked out to Richey's horse. The boy was hunched in the saddle, taking the punishment of the long ride with a stoicism David would not have suspected he possessed.

Townsend asked, "A brush with Union troops?"

Luther Lusk took it upon himself to answer. "No, sir, it was Comanchero traders. We put in at a tradin' post north of here." His eyes met David's. "That was a mistake."

"I know the people," Townsend said with bitterness. His gaze landed upon Floyd Bearfield. He took a startled step backward, then hatred filled his face. "Is that where you got *him*?"

Lusk nodded, mildly surprised at Townsend's reaction. "Yes, sir. Picked us up a prize, didn't we?"

Townsend noted with evident approval the rope around Bearfield's neck. "If you are looking for a place to tie the other end of it, there are some good strong trees down on the river. I'd be glad to escort you down there personally. In fact, I'd take it as a personal favor."

Lusk looked coolly at David. "I'd be pleasured, myself. But the lieutenant is given to makin' promises."

Townsend turned back to David. "Lieutenant, my invitation extends to you and all your Texans. It does not extend to that man. If he makes any attempt to set foot inside my home, I'll be obliged to kill him!"

Bearfield was anxious. "You promised me, Buckalew. I brought you here. Now turn me loose."

"When I'm ready." David shifted his attention to Townsend. "Bearfield is our prisoner, sir. You'll have to indulge us a little. We'll not impose on your hospitality any further than we have to."

Townsend said firmly, "I don't know what promises you've made, but I hope you're a practical man. I hope you recognize realities. Your word to a man like this is nothing, because *he* is nothing."

David thought, *If it's my word, it remains my word no matter who I give it to.* But he kept the thought to himself. He had more important business on his mind than to argue morality with a Yankee.

The corner of his eye caught a movement, and he quickly turned his head. A young woman stepped through the arch, shading her eyes with her hand. The wind caught her long skirt and boogered a couple of the nearest horses. She picked out Pete Richey and walked toward him.

Something about her jolted David. For a moment it was as if he knew her, as if the sight of her tried to summon up a memory hidden deeply in some dark recess of his mind. He stared, puzzled. There was no way he could ever have known this woman.

Her eyes were cold as she studied the boy slumped in the saddle. "How many of our men did he kill before they got him?"

David couldn't find voice to answer her.

Owen Townsend said, "It wasn't our men. He was wounded in a brush with Floyd Bearfield's people."

The name Bearfield seemed to hit her like a fist. She turned quickly, her eyes wide as she looked at Townsend. "They fought with Bearfield?"

Owen Townsend pointed. "He's their prisoner, Martha."

Her face seemed to drain of color as she saw Bearfield for the first time. Her hands lifted involuntarily to cover her mouth, as if to keep her from crying out. They turned to fists, and she suddenly ran forward, holding the fists together and using them to beat at Bearfield. She screamed at him.

Bearfield tried to pull back but was hemmed in. "Will somebody get this crazy woman away from me?"

The men were too startled to do anything except watch her. Owen Townsend stepped forward and grasped his daughter's shoulder. He pulled her around. "It'll be all right, girl. He's their prisoner."

She laid her head against his chest, her shoulders trembling. He held her with his good arm and said, "I apologize for my daughter. But she has good reason. We both do."

When she gained control, she turned again. Her eyes purposely avoided Bearfield. "Where's that wounded boy? Let's get him into the house where we can tend to him."

Luther Lusk and Gene Ivy lifted Richey down from the saddle. Carefully they carried him through the arch and toward the adobe building, following the fast-walking girl.

David stared after them, taken totally by surprise. It took him a minute to recover and get back to the pressing business. He found Townsend staring at Bearfield again, the hatred strong.

"Mister Townsend, how many people do you have here?"

"No Union troops, Lieutenant."

"How many of your own people?"

Warily Townsend hedged. "If I told you that, then you would know as much as I do."

"I *need* to know as much as you do, at least on this subject."

"I needn't remind you, Lieutenant, that we are on opposite sides. I'll give you whatever aid I can in a humanitarian way, and see you started on south. But that's as far as I can go."

David's voice firmed. "How many people, Mister Townsend?"

Townsend considered a moment, then relented, evidently seeing no way the information could be of great value to the enemy. "Just a few of us . . . my daughter . . . half a dozen Mexican ranchhands. Three of the men are married and have wives and children here. There's an old Mexican woman, too, mother to one of the men. She helps my daughter in the house."

"And *Mrs*. Townsend?"

Townsend seemed to flinch. "She's up the hill yonder. Buried."

"Oh. I'm sorry." David frowned, not fully trusting. "Doesn't seem like many people for a place of this size."

"We went north last year when you Texans came. Most of our help scattered. The thieves—red *and* white—took off a big part of our cattle. We haven't been back long enough to get our help together again." He added pensively, "As you've surely noted by now, Lieutenant, war is a very expensive enterprise. I wish we could get by without it."

"We didn't ask for it either."

"Then who did? I keep asking myself."

Townsend started toward the patio entrance. "I'll get some women commenced cooking. We don't have much except beef. I imagine you'll be anxious to get on your way. You never know when Union troops may show up." The last, David thought, was said hopefully.

David followed him into the shade of the patio. "You're a long way from any real settlement here."

Townsend considered, suspicious of the comment. "Tolerably."

"Come right down to cases, you're pretty far out onto Indian territory. How do you manage to keep your scalp on?"

"With care, Lieutenant." Townsend gazed back out the archway toward the spread of far blue mountains and across the valley that was beginning to show the first tinge of green for an observer who used imagination. "Out here you don't look to other people to help you much; you take care of yourself. Government means little to you . . . Mexican, American, Confederate . . . You fight your own battles or avoid them. You make your own treaties, your own compromises. I've lived around Indians for most of thirty years. I came out here in the early times and trapped beaver when this was still part of Mexico. A man had to be watchful then. If he got careless his scalp wound up on an Indian lance or he wound up in a Mexican prison. I learned to be watchful and to get along. I've made my own treaties and kept them, even when armies couldn't do it. The only real trouble I've had has been from men like Bearfield, who know no truth and no law."

David did not try to hold back his curiosity. "What did Bearfield do to you, sir?"

Townsend's face pinched. An old anger was in his eyes. But he said only, "Enough." He knotted his good hand into a fist. "You wouldn't think so now, but he was a soldier once. I knew him then. He was an army supply officer, and a good one until he became addicted to some of the major vices.

You can't afford those on military pay. He began converting government supplies to his own use. Some army rifles fell into Indian hands and were traced back to him. He deserted just ahead of a court-martial. I suppose his skill as a supply officer has been of good use to him in his present trade." Townsend looked around. "When you're through with him, I don't suppose you would turn him over to me?"

"For the U.S. Army?"

"No. Just for me."

David shook his head. "No sir, I reckon not." He followed Townsend through a doorway and into what he found was a parlor. The adobe wall, he noted, was fully two feet thick. He stopped and measured the door facing with his hand.

Townsend said, "We built the place to last through my grandchildren's time."

"How many do you have?"

A momentary sadness passed over Townsend's face. "None." He turned away. David sensed that he had touched him where he hurt.

Women's voices were speaking Spanish in the next room. David walked to the doorway to look. Pete Richey lay on a cot. His shirt had been removed. Luther Lusk stood holding it, evidently waiting for orders from the Townsend girl. Martha Townsend, wearing a white apron tied snugly around a slender waist, was washing Richey's chest and shoulders with a large wet cloth. By the smell of it, David judged she was using alcohol. Her hands were gentle but sure.

The setting and the smell took him back. For a moment he was in the makeshift military hospital in Albuquerque, trying to fight his way through a painful fog to the light, trying to see the faces of the people who hovered over him, the people to whom belonged the hands which worked on him as Martha Townsend's worked on Pete Richey now. David thought of a girl he had seen so dimly, a girl whose hands had been gentle but whose face had been a blur to him, a girl he had wished ever afterward that he might see again, to know if she was really as beautiful as she had seemed.

He studied Martha Townsend, wondering if Pete Richey saw her now as David had seen that girl in Albuquerque. David saw her clearly enough to know she was not beautiful. He was not sure he would even call her pretty. Perhaps he might, if he had not seen the snap of hostility in those blue eyes as she had first stepped out of the house and looked upon the Texans.

Joshua Buckalew had admonished him never to judge by beautiful features or beautiful skin. Real beauty, real character was to be found in the eyes, he had said. *The eyes tell the truth when the face lies.*

She noticed him standing in the door and gave him an impatient flash of those blue eyes, seeming to suggest that he find gainful employment elsewhere.

David said to Owen Townsend, "This is not a job I enjoy pushin' off onto a woman."

"She knows what she's doing. She was a volunteer in the military hospital while we were in Albuquerque."

David frowned. *Could it have been her after all?* Somehow he hoped not. The dream had been a thing of beauty to him, one of the few good things he had found in all these months in New Mexico. That girl across the room fell far short of the dream.

He watched her skillful hands wrap a fresh bandage securely around Richey's wound. A Mexican woman helped, handing her what she asked for. Luther Lusk turned Richey partway over when Martha Townsend told him to.

David held silent until the job was done. "What about Pete? How's he goin' to be?"

She only glanced at David, then looked back at the boy. "He should live, I think, if you don't kill him making him ride. But I suppose you will. Taken as a whole, Texans are a thoughtless lot, from what I've seen of them. The Union should have been glad to let you secede, and good riddance."

David forced down the quick anger that stirred in him. Anger was of no use to him here. *Attitudes like hers were the reason for this war in the first place,* he thought.

She said, "It's time we all got out of here and let this young man have some rest. We can't go with you standing in the middle of the door."

David quickly stepped aside. Thinking about it then, he wished he had taken more time. It would have been more seemly. What galled him most, he thought, was that Luther Lusk had seen him move at the girl's command.

But Lusk showed no sign that he had noticed. He seemed pleased. "Looks like old Pete's goin' to make it."

The girl nodded. "But he'll need a lot of rest."

David shook his head. "I'm afraid he can't rest long. We have to be movin' south pretty soon."

"You could leave him here. He would be well cared for."

"And be a prisoner the first time Union troops came by."

"Hardly anyone ever comes by, Lieutenant."

"*We* did. And chances are good that we're bein' trailed by Union cavalry. I wouldn't like the thought of that boy spendin' the rest of the war in a Union prison."

A dark humor came briefly into the girl's eyes. "When we were in Albuquerque I heard some of you Texans brag that the war wouldn't last three months."

David felt anger stirring again. He tried not to give her the satisfaction of seeing him rise to the bait. "I'm surprised you'd even offer to keep Richey here and take care of him, as little as you think of Texans."

"Your Mister Lusk told me about the skirmish with the Bearfield people. That helps outweigh the fact that you're Texans. Incidentally, he mentioned that you didn't take part in it."

David flinched.

She went on, "Anyway, this boy is wounded. That makes him different."

"*I* was wounded, once." He said it with a motive, thinking perhaps she would look closer, perhaps recognize him.

She showed no sign that she did. "Evidently you got over it."

Owen Townsend seemed to decide his daughter had said enough. "Martha, I wish you would get a few of the women together and start cooking up something for these men, so they can be on their way."

She protested, "You know that boy in there needs rest."

"They may *all* have a long rest if Union cavalry should find them here. We don't want this place turned into a battleground."

David said, "Neither do we. That's why we'll stay no
longer than absolutely necessary. The cooking can wait,
Mister Townsend. Right now I'll have to ask you to get all of
your people outside."

Townsend's eyes showed alarm. "What are you going to
do?"

"We won't harm anybody unless we're forced to it. But
we need to have all your people outside where we can watch
them."

Townsend demanded stiffly, "Watch them do *what*? Nobody here is going to make any move against you or your
men."

"I hope not, because we've got to search your place."

Townsend darkened. "This is a gross abuse of our hospitality."

Martha Townsend's face was flushed crimson, her arms
folded tightly across her breasts.

In a few minutes the ranch people were gathered in the
open patio. Most were fearful, a couple of the Mexican men
belligerent, looking to Owen Townsend for leadership.
David sensed that if Townsend gave the word, they would
put up a fight. David counted and tried to remember just
how many people Towsend had told him there were. "Is this
all of them?"

Townsend's civility was gone. Tautly he said, "All but two
men out on horseback, looking for cattle. They'll be in before dark."

David took him at his word; he could do little else. He
turned toward his own men, who were watching the Townsend people distrustfully. "Now I want you all to spread out
and go through the house. You know what you're lookin' for.
That's *all* you're lookin' for, except guns. Whatever guns you
find, bring them out."

His gaze swept their faces. Whatever he might think of
them in other respects, he had no reason to believe any of
his men were thieves. As the soldiers disappeared into the
house, David turned back to Townsend. "My apologies, sir.
This is my first war. I've already found out we have to do
things we'd rather not do."

Martha Townsend demanded, "What do you think you'll find in there? Do you think we've hidden a troop of Union soldiers?"

David looked her straight in the eye. "I think you know what we're lookin' for, Miss Townsend. Your father does."

He saw the quick look that passed between father and daughter. Up to that moment he was not certain that she did know. Now there was no question in his mind. He said, "I wouldn't insult you by askin' you to tell us where to look, Mister Townsend. We'll find it ourselves without compromise to your patriotism."

Martha Townsend said harshly, "That is very considerate."

"Your father can take comfort in knowin' we didn't find out through him."

He could see the question burning in Townsend's eyes: how *had* they found out? But to ask would be to admit of knowledge. Townsend held silent.

Floyd Bearfield leaned against the wall in a corner of the patio. Fermin Hernandez had remained to keep him under guard. Hernandez kept his rifle aimed loosely in Bearfield's direction, not directly at him but close enough that Bearfield could not forget about it for a minute. Bearfield studied David and Townsend with much curiosity. He never had been told why the Texans were looking for the Townsend ranch; he still didn't know. David saw no point in telling him.

In a little while the soldiers began coming back emptyhanded. David counted them off, one by one. His confidence, at a high point when the search had started, began to ebb sharply. The last one out was Noley Mitchell. The old peace officer shook his head. "Sorry, Davey, but it looks like we've come up dry."

Uneasily David protested, "It's got to be here. Maybe there's a cellar under the house."

"We found the cellar all right. There wasn't nothin' in it but some supplies of one kind and another. No munitions."

Bearfield pushed away from the wall and stood straight, suddenly highly interested. His lips formed the word "munitions," though he did not speak aloud.

Luther Lusk spat. "I could of told you we wouldn't find no such thing in the house, or under it either. If somethin' had ever touched it off, there wouldn't of been enough left of this place to build a chicken coop. If there ever *was* any munitions—which I doubt—they've hidden them someplace out away from here."

"It's here," David argued. "If it wasn't here they wouldn't have sent a Union detail out to recover it."

Townsend's jaw dropped. "Detail? What's this about a Union detail?"

David considered before answering. "I don't guess there's any reason we oughtn't to tell you. Indians wiped out a Union detail. I found a letter on the officer." He fished the letter from his pocket and read the first part to Townsend. The ranchman clenched his fist.

David said, "I didn't intend to ask you, Mister Townsend, but now I've got to. Where is that cache at?"

Townsend looked at him with a strong measure of doubt. "You sure it was Indians? You sure *you* didn't do it?"

"It was Indians."

Townsend was frowning. "We're in a war, Lieutenant, and you're my enemy. If I told you anything, that would be treason . . . giving aid and comfort."

David's fists knotted in frustration. He wished he knew the man well enough to be aware of a weakness. "Mister Townsend, if I had more time I might be able to play with you, but I don't. I'm askin' you again."

Townsend gave no ground. David looked at the Mexicans, wondering which of them might be easiest to break.

Townsend was ahead of him. "No use wasting your time on my people. They know nothing. They had no part in it. Even if you tortured them, there's nothing they can tell you."

David took him at his word. "Then, that just leaves you."

Martha Townsend said bitterly, "There's also *me*. Why don't you torture *me*, Lieutenant?"

Owen Townsend turned on his daughter. "This one time you'd better hold your tongue, girl. It could get you into more trouble than you can handle."

She started to say more, but David cut her short. "I was taught a long time ago—honor thy father."

Sarcastically she said, "So you know a little Scripture . . . somehow I'm surprised."

"This might be a good time for a little Scripture. We're on serious business here. We mean to find that cache."

But the determined look in the Townsends' eyes told him he wasn't going to find it by asking them. And he and his men didn't have time to dig holes all over this ranch.

Floyd Bearfield took a step forward. "You never have asked *me*, Buckalew." He had an air of confidence he hadn't shown since losing the advantage at the trading post.

"What do you know about it?" David asked, suspicious.

"I know things about this ranch that you wouldn't find out if you prowled around here for a month. And you don't have a month."

"You know where the stuff is hidden?"

"I know a logical place where it *might* be hidden."

David saw a flicker of concern in Townsend's eyes. That was enough. "Go on, then. Tell me what you know."

Bearfield shook his head. "Not that easy, Texan. I don't just give it to you. I trade."

"Trade for what?"

"Freedom."

"I've already promised you freedom."

"I want a good fast horse to be sure I can keep that freedom after you've delivered it." He glanced at Townsend; murder was in the rancher's eyes. Bearfield said, "You see why I need the horse."

"You'll have time to get away."

"But I want something else, too. I want a percentage of the goods."

David shook his head. "A horse, but no percentage."

Bearfield asked, "How much munitions do you expect to find?"

David didn't answer.

Bearfield said, "It must be a fair amount if you're willing to go to so much trouble for it. You could spare me some.

We need it, the business we're in, the people we deal with
It's a dangerous life."

"A lot *more* dangerous for the people you come across
No guns or ammunition for you, Bearfield. Just the horse.

"I don't see that you're in a position to argue. You can'
afford to go hunting for it; you're fighting against time. An'
hour now, Union soldiers may come riding over that hill."

David couldn't help himself; he glanced at the hill ove
which he and his men had come.

Luther Lusk scowled at Bearfield. "Lieutenant, if you'c
just turn him over to me and the boys, I believe we coulc
persuade him to take a more liberal view."

It was the first time, offhand, that David could remembe
agreeing with Lusk. He gave the matter some considera
tion.

Bearfield discerned the drift of David's thinking. "Yo
promised. You promised you'd set me free."

David looked him in the eye. "I'm a horse trader by pro
fession. Horse traders have been known to lie. Sure,
promised to set you free. But I didn't promise I'd keep
some of my men from trailin' right after you. I'll give yo
freedom, but it'll be up to you to try and keep it."

Luther Lusk rubbed his powerful right fist into the paln
of his left hand. "Give him his freedom now, Buckalew. Giv
him a hundred yards head start."

Bearfield seemed to wilt a little. He could see that Davic
was considering the proposition seriously. "All right, no
share. Just the horse. And nobody follows after me, is tha
agreed? Nobody follows after me."

"I can't speak for anybody but my men and me. *We* won'
come after you. What Townsend and his people do is some
thin' I can't control after we leave here. You'll have a goo
head start."

"An hour. Give me an hour on Townsend and I'll make i
from there."

Townsend warned, "You'd better think hard before you
make promises to him, Buckalew. He might be lucky anc
find some of his Indian friends out yonder. He would turr
around and come after you."

"Do *you* want to tell me where the goods are hidden, Mister Townsend? Then I wouldn't have to trade with him at all."

Townsend paced in a tight circle, brooding. "You know I can't do that." David gave him a little time, hoping the rancher might weaken. Townsend halted and looked back at him. "Lieutenant, I'm not admitting to anything. But if there *were* a store of goods such as you're talking about, what could you do with it? You couldn't haul it away from here on horseback. There's no way you could get any good from it."

"I'm not worried about gettin' any good from it, sir. All I intend to do is to take the harm out of it. I'm goin' to blow it up."

Bearfield protested, "Blow it up? Good God, man, do you have any idea what that stuff is worth today?"

David brought his hand up to his half-healed arm and replied with bitterness, "I know what it's worth, turned against my people."

"I'll buy it from you, Buckalew. Depending on how much of it there is, I'll pay you in gold, and I'll swear to you that no Union troops will ever use a pound of it."

"And what would you do with it, Bearfield? How many stolen cattle and horses would the Comanches trade you for it? How many stolen Mexican girls? And you know what the Indians would do with those goods. They would raid down into lower Texas, and plumb into Mexico, to bring you *more* stolen goods. And how many of my people would they kill in the process?" He knotted his fists and took a step forward. "You said you'd take us to it. Do it now or I turn you loose with a hundred-yard start . . . afoot!"

Bearfield sullenly gave in. He pointed his chin. "Yonder, down the river. There's a cave down there, a big one."

"A cave?"

"Indian traders used to store goods in it before Townsend came here and took over this part of the country for himself."

Anger boiled in Townsend's eyes. David sensed that Bearfield had struck upon the truth.

Townsend's voice was barbed with fury. "I already owe you for blood, Bearfield. Now I owe you for treason." He turned away, his face dark. With his back to David he said, "You've found out what you wanted to know, Lieutenant. Now I'd be obliged if you'd get that man away from here. I can't stand to look at him or to smell him."

David should have felt exhilaration, but he didn't. He felt like a participant in some dark and unsavory conspiracy. "Mister Townsend, under better circumstances . . ." He let it trail off, hoping Townsend would know what he meant to say.

Townsend still didn't look at him. "Am I a prisoner, or am I free to go back into my house?"

"It's your house. But I'll ask you not to leave it."

David saw a grin on Luther Lusk's face. For the first time, this contrary frontiersman was beginning to believe. And he saw a gleam of approval in the eyes of Noley Mitchell. "Davey," the sergeant said, "you just may make an officer yet."

David didn't have time to bask in the glow of this unaccustomed approval. He turned to Lusk. "I want you to stay here with most of the men and watch over things."

Lusk shook his head. "No siree, Buckalew. I'm goin' to take a look in that cave."

"I'm givin' you an order, Lusk."

"And I'm tellin' you to take your order and go to hell with it."

The two men glared, each waiting for the other to back down. David said, "When we get back to Texas, you'll have a lot to answer for."

"We ain't there yet by a good ways."

The farm boy, Gene Ivy, volunteered, "Lieutenant, I'll stay here and watch after things."

David realized he could not let the thing pass; Lusk had challenged him, and he must meet that challenge if he expected to keep any discipline in this command until he could get the men safely home. He kept his eyes grimly on Lusk, finding no evidence that the frontiersman was going to back away. He slowly drew his pistol from its holster and brought it up to bear on Lusk. "I gave you an order."

Lusk tried to hold his gaze on David's eyes, but finally he was forced to look down at the pistol. David knew then that he had him. He held his hand rock-steady. Lusk looked back into David's eyes and swore under his breath. "You'd do it. I believe, by God, you'd do it."

"I'd do it."

Noley Mitchell decided it was time to take a hand. "Luther, we've got more to do than watch you try to match determination with the lieutenant. If he says stay, I reckon you'll stay and try to act like it was your idea in the first place."

Lusk hunched. "I was just tryin' him out."

The sergeant impatiently shook his head. "Looks to me like you'd get tired of that. You've already found out he'll do what he says he will."

"*You* wouldn't shoot a man like that, would you, Noley?"

"I don't know. I ain't a lieutenant."

David wished at that moment that Mitchell *were* the lieutenant. But he could see that Lusk's resistance was over. How many more tests would he have to surmount before he could get these men home and rid himself of this unwanted responsibility?

Gene Ivy said again, "Lieutenant, I'll stay here."

The lad's eagerness to please somehow lifted a little of the burden and made David's spirits rise a little. "Thanks, Ivy." He looked around. "Where's Homer Gilman?" The tall miller stepped out from behind some of the other men. "Here, Lieutenant."

"Gilman, I'm leaving' you in charge. I want you to post guards around the place and see that no civilians leave here till we've finished the job. I don't want them findin' help and bringin' it down on top of us. Other than that, you don't hurt anybody and you don't bother anything. Is that clear?"

Gilman looked at Mitchell, then said, "Sure is, Lieutenant."

David, Mitchell and Hernandez saw to their horses. Two other men, the immigrants O'Shea and Hufstedler, were picked to go along. Mitchell said to the Irishman, "Patrick, there is a rope on Smith's saddle. I wish you would put a loop around Bearfield's neck."

The Irishman hummed some kind of a chanty as he moved gladly to comply. Bearfield's eyes narrowed resentfully as the rope was placed around his neck. O'Shea drew it up tighter than was necessary, enough perhaps to give Bearfield's skin a burn. The man flinched and started to voice a protest but thought better of it and said nothing. He slouched in the saddle, smoldering.

They rode down to the river, the Texans and Floyd Bearfield. Then they turned south, following the flow of the water. Half a mile down, Bearfield pointed. "That's it, just under that little bluff."

David squinted. At first he didn't see it and suspected that Bearfield lied. When he finally spotted it he realized how easily he could have ridden past without discovering it. A scattering of low brush obscured the opening.

Bearfield said, "An old Mexican told me he hid in there once for two days from some Indians who had bought bad whisky from him. They were from out on the plains and didn't know this piece of country. Afterwards he used this place to hide his trade goods."

Riding up to the cave, David decided it would have been feasible for the Yankees to bring their wagons within twenty or thirty feet of the small opening. They wouldn't have to carry the goods by hand very far. He dismounted. The opening was large enough that he could walk into it by bending at the waist; he wouldn't have to get on his knees and crawl.

Noley Mitchell stared speculatively at the cave. David was mildly surprised to see a stirring of excitement in the sergeant's eyes. "By God, there *is* a cave," Mitchell said.

"You doubted it?"

"To be honest with you, Davey, I've doubted this whole thing all along. It's been such a long time since I've seen anything work out right in this crazy country . . ."

"You saw the Yankee letter."

"Saw it, but somehow I couldn't ever quite believe in it. I guess I figured when we got here we'd find that the Yankees had already taken everything away, if they had ever left it here in the first place. You've been away from home long enough to see how armies operate. One hand never knows what the other hand is up to. Mostly they just stumble along like a man in the dark and hope the other side stumbles worse."

David said, "We found the cave, but we still don't know if there's really anything in it."

Mitchell nodded. "You want me to go in first?"

"No, I'll go."

"I'd move a little slow, was I you. For all you know a bear might've taken a likin' to it, or a mountain lion. They may not take a likin' to *you*."

"Then you'd be rid of me."

"You think the boys would breathe easier for that?"

"I know they would."

He handed his reins to O'Shea and told him to keep an eye on Bearfield. "Hufstedler, you go up on top and keep a lookout. Hernandez, you go upriver a ways and watch. We don't want anybody slippin' up on us."

Bearfield said sullenly, "I've done everything you brought me for. I've shown you the ranch, and I've shown you the cave. It's time you turned me loose."

"When I'm ready."

Bearfield glared at him in hatred. "You don't intend to turn me loose. You're goin' to kill me, or let Owen Townsend do it."

It wasn't in Bearfield's nature to trust anyone, or to accept a promise for what it was, David decided.

"Bad as I hate to," he said, "I promised to turn you loose, and I will. But in *my* time, not in yours."

He stooped and moved slowly into the gloom of the cave, sniffing for animal scent that might indicate he was not alone. He found only the dry smell of ancient dust, bitter to his nostrils. It seemed to rise up each time he moved his feet. He heard a noise and turned quickly, half expecting something to jump at him. Noley Mitchell had followed him into the cave.

David paused, letting his eyes adjust slowly to the poor light. He could get no clear idea of the cave's size. Farther back the ceiling appeared high enough that he could stand erect. Wind never reached far into this cave, and moisture never touched it. He saw old boot tracks in the dust, disturbed only by a crisscrossing of newer animal tracks. Beyond them was a dark and shapeless bulk, covered in grayed tarpaulins. David wished for a torch that he might see better, but he knew that was a foolish notion. If this *was* the cache, one spark in the wrong place would blow him and the others to the far side of the Pecos River.

He found the corner of a tarp and raised it. Behind it was a stack of kegs. He rolled one out and saw the word painted on it: *powder*.

He forgot about dignity and decorum. He forgot all the rules that had been drilled into him about proper conduct for an officer and a gentleman. He whooped loudly and danced half a dozen jig steps across the dusty floor.

A voice from the cave opening said, "Noley, I do believe the boy's human after all."

Luther Lusk was standing there. David started to ask how, but he already knew. He said, "You just don't follow orders, do you?"

Lusk shook his head. "Not worth a damn." He took several strides across the dusty floor and threw the tarp back farther. He glanced at the sergeant, his eyes wide with surprise. "You see that, Noley? By God, the kid was right all the time. It's here. It's here!" He turned to David. "How much of it is there?"

"They're supposed to be sendin' ten wagons for it."

"Ten wagons." Lusk stared at the cache with those dark hawk eyes and rubbed his mouth and chin fiercely.

David said, "Lusk, as long as you're here you'd just as well set in to makin' a hand. Let's roll a few of those powder barrels out. We'll make a trail of powder across the floor and down toward the river. That'll give us time to get clear before the whole thing goes up."

Lusk blinked. "Ten wagonloads. That's enough to move this hillside down and dam up the whole Pecos River."

David nodded. "Then Mister Townsend will have himself a real fine lake."

"Maybe right up into his bedroom."

David repeated, "Lusk, let's get movin' with those barrels."

Noley Mitchell had been staring silently at the cache. He held up the palm of his hand. "Let's wait a minute, Davey. I think maybe we ought to stop and talk this thing over."

David looked at him, puzzling. "I don't see how we can go wrong. It'll be the easiest thing in the world to touch it off."

"I wasn't thinkin' about touchin' it off, Davey. I was thinkin' about *not* touchin' it off."

"We've got to. You know how much damage the Yankees can do us with all this stuff."

"If they get it. But it occurs to me that they don't have to get it, and we don't have to blow it up, either. Instead of the Yankees usin' this against us, we could use it against them. All we've got to do is haul it out of here to where it'll do us the most good."

David blinked in surprise. "How? On horseback? We couldn't carry enough with us to spike a cannon. Townsend doesn't have but one decent wagon that I saw. I'd figured to take that with us to haul Pete Richey."

"Accordin' to your letter the Yankees are sendin' ten wagons. We could just wait and use those."

"The wagons aren't comin' by themselves. There'll be soldiers with them, maybe a lot of soldiers."

"Strategy, Davey. When the other side's got the biggest strength you use strategy. I'll bet if we put our heads together we can figure out a way to persuade them Yanks around to our way of thinkin'."

David turned and looked at the large store of munitions. For just a wild moment . . ."

Mitchell kept pressing him. "Ten wagonloads of shot and shell. Think on it, Davey. A whole damned war could be fought with that, if we could get it to the right place and at the right time."

The notion was contagious. David let his imagination run unbridled. For a moment he pictured a narrow pass, perhaps somewhere to the south, an entrapment like the Yankees had made against the Texans in Apache Canyon, except that this time it would be the other way around, the

Yankee Army being euchered into a trap from which they couldn't escape.

Mitchell said, "We been goin' towards home with our tails between our legs. You think you're the only man in this outfit who's felt that way, Davey? We've all felt it. Now here we stand, lookin' at a chance to stay in the fight after all. We've got one last chance to come out of this thing with some dignity and pride. Hell, who knows? If everything broke for us just right we might even turn this war around and start a whole new push to the north again. We might drive them people clear back into Colorado, and back out to California. We almost done it once. Who's to say we couldn't do it again with a little luck? A little luck and ten wagonloads of ammunition?"

The vision was staggering. The temptation was almost overwhelming.

Almost. But David saw the flaw. "There's too many *ifs* in it, Sergeant. It works *if* we can take the wagons away from the Yankees. It works *if* some other Yankee force doesn't catch up to us before we can get clear of the country. But supposin' one of those *ifs* goes against us? The Yankees recover the whole thing, and we've made this trip for nothin'. Some of us—probably most of us—will die, wasted. No, it's safer to do what we came here for. Blow it up." He turned to roll out a barrel of powder.

He heard a shot. For a second he froze, thinking this whole cache was about to explode, with him and the others on top of it.

Lusk declared, "Outside! Somethin's gone wrong outside!" He stooped and rushed back out through the opening. David sprinted across the cave. As he went, he heard another shot, and still another.

The sunlight blinded him for a moment. He saw Lusk standing with his arm outstretched, trying to take aim at something moving. Lusk's pistol roared.

Floyd Bearfield was getting away.

From on top of the hill, Hufstedler fired his rifle as Bearfield came into his view. It was a forlorn hope; David had been told Hufstedler was the poorest shot in the command.

David called for him to cease fire. He turned, knowing what he would find and dreading it.

Patrick O'Shea lay in a spreading pool of his own blood. He coughed painfully, struggling for breath. David could tell at a glance that he had few left to him.

"I'm sorry," O'Shea rasped. "I tried . . . to look in the cave . . . He . . . surprised me . . ."

Luther Lusk and Fermin Hernandez had spurred after Bearfield, but David knew the chase was hopeless. Bearfield had too long a start. He cursed softly. "He didn't have to do this. I was goin' to turn him loose."

Mitchell said, "*He* didn't believe that."

"But I was . . ."

Hufstedler half slid, half ran down the hill, shouting, "Patrick! Patrick!" From where he had been he probably could not have seen what was happening down here. David had sent him up there for a better view of different terrain. The German stopped, staring with wide eyes, then dropped to his knees beside the dying Irishman. "Damn you, Patrick," he said thickly, tears streaking his cheeks, "I ought to kick for you your butt! What for you let him shoot you?"

O'Shea was past answering him, or even hearing. He lived a few more minutes, gradually falling back farther and farther beyond reach. The breathing stopped, and the only sound was from Hufstedler, alternately crying out in grief and in rage.

Hernandez and Lusk came back in a little while, their horses lathered from the fruitless run. Lusk's face was dark with frustration. "He lost us over in them hills. He knows them, and we don't."

David turned to Noley Mitchell. "It was a great notion, Sergeant, for a few minutes. But now we've *got* to blow up that cache."

"I don't see why."

"Bearfield will listen for the explosion. If he doesn't hear it he'll pretty soon figure out what we're up to. He wants that stuff as much as we do. He'll come after it sooner or later. We're just seventeen men now, sixteen when you

count out Pete Richey. We can't fight off Yankees and Bearfield both."

Mitchell looked at Lusk, who knew what he was talking
about, and at Hernandez, who hadn't heard any of the earlier conversation. "There might be a bunch of us willin' to
try."

"Not at the risk of lettin' these goods fall into the wrong
hands. We're goin' to set fire to it and run like hell." He
turned and started back for the mouth of the cave. He heard
a few half-whispered words pass between Mitchell and
Lusk. Someone stepped up quickly behind him. David felt
something poke him in the back.

Lusk's voice spoke firmly, "You'd best raise your hands,
Buckalew. I'm takin' the borry of your pistol."

David stiffened. He might have expected many things,
but not this. He lifted his hands and felt the pistol being
drawn from his holster. He turned, easing his hands down,
knowing they wouldn't likely shoot him. Lusk still had a
pistol aimed his way and held David's pistol loosely in his
left hand.

David turned accusing eyes at Noley Mitchell. The sergeant stood straight, his jaw grim and determined.

"Sergeant," David said, "I wouldn't be surprised at anything from Lusk. But *you* . . ."

"Sorry, Davey. But this time I reckon we're goin' to have
to do things my way."

David looked to Hernandez and Hufstedler. Neither
comprehended the run of events, but neither showed any
disposition to help David. He knew their first loyalty was to
Mitchell. Both seemed to be waiting for the sergeant to
explain.

David looked into the muzzle of Lusk's pistol and shivered involuntarily. He was not afraid; he was confident that
nobody intended to kill him unless he crowded them into
it. More than anything he felt frustration. Everything had
gone sour in this damned war, for the Texas forces in general
and for him individually. He hadn't wanted to be put in
charge of this detail in the first place, and he had never
been able to win anything better from most of the men than
a grudging tolerance. Now even that little seemed lost.

He said tautly, "This is rebellion."

Lusk replied, "I thought that's what the whole war is."

Noley Mitchell motioned for Lusk to lower the pistol. "No need to point that thing at him, Luther. It might go off."

David turned to Mitchell. "This'll go hard with you, Sergeant, when we get back to Texas."

Mitchell smiled, a little. "Davey, you're young, and I make allowances for the young. Time a man's my age he's seen most of what the world has to offer, and seen *through* a lot of it. You're too young to've seen through much. They make all them fancy speeches and tell you how it's supposed to be, and it's too much to expect of a young feller to know what's real and what's talk. They tell you you're an officer and a gentleman, and that everybody else has to obey you because they've put a gold bar on your coat. That's all right, when everything is goin' the way it ought to. But there comes a time, when nothin' goes right, that somebody has to step in and show you what the real world is."

"And you've taken it on yourself to do that?"

Mitchell nodded regretfully. "I've stood by you and done what I could to keep you from makin' any real bad mistakes. And I'll have to say that, considerin' your limited experience, you ain't done bad at all. But this time I believe you're wrong. I believe we've got a good chance here to strike a blow for Texas. Since you *don't* believe it, I've got to bring you around to my way of thinkin', or I've got to take the command away from you."

"Looks to me like you've already done that."

"Maybe. Maybe not. It depends on you."

"You mean you'd give the command back to me, provided I do what you tell me to?"

"Somethin' like that."

"It wouldn't really be command then, would it?"

"Nobody ever has total command, except for God. I have no wish to shame or belittle you, Davey. But I want us to take this chance for the good of Texas. For the good of the men in this detail. For me and you."

"It's a long risk. If it doesn't work, how is it for the good of any of us?"

Mitchell's eyes took on an intensity David had not seen in them before. "You've never really thought much of these men, have you?"

David hesitated about answering, then decided the truth probably showed anyway. "No, I can't say I've been much impressed."

"This was a good outfit, a better one than you can imagine. Every man in this bunch thought the world of old Lieutenant Satterwhite. All he had to do was snap his fingers and everybody was lined up and ready for whatever come. We always said we'd ride into hell if he led us." A remembered sadness touched Mitchell. "And that's what happened, finally. We rode into hell, and a lot of the men didn't come out again. Satterwhite, God bless him, was the first to fall because he was out in front, where he always was. It's taken a lot out of this crew, gettin' whipped like we did. Maybe it was the same in the outfit *you* was with."

David didn't answer, but he remembered.

Mitchell looked upriver, the painful memories pinching his eyes. "The spirit was gone. I kept hopin' we'd get it back. When I found out they didn't intend to let the men elect a new officer for themselves, I at least hoped they'd give us one who could lead us the way *he* did. Well, they gave us you." Mitchell turned his gaze back half apologetically to David. "I ain't sayin' you haven't tried; you have. I ain't sayin' that under better circumstances you wouldn't be a good officer, even for this bunch. But you joined us when the men was already feelin' whipped, and we ain't done a thing since but retreat or get chased halfway across New Mexico. All we've had is dirt and sweat and fleas. It ain't your fault, it's just how things go.

"Now we've got one chance to win back that spirit we had, to stir up the pride we lost. I intend to see us get that chance. *With* you, if you'll agree. *Without* you, if you don't."

"What'll you do if I don't? Shoot me?"

Mitchell frowned. "No, we'd let you go on south without us. Anybody who feels like he don't want to be part of what we're fixin' to do, he can ride along with you. If you won't help us, we don't want you in our way." He stared at David a moment. "Davey, I ain't told you, but I met your old daddy once. I think I know how you've tried to live up to him. I'm wonderin' how you'd feel—how *he'd* feel—if you rode back to Texas by yourself, and we come along later with that whole wagon train of war goods?"

David looked away from the sergeant, afraid his thoughts would show. Mitchell had stepped on him where his foot was sorest. Joshua Buckalew had won *his* war. Worst of all to David these past weeks had been the realization that he was going home a loser.

He said, "There are just so many things that could go wrong . . ."

"You ain't a coward, Davey. I think I know you well enough to be sure of that."

"I've already told you what I'm scaredest of. If this doesn't work, everything falls back into the hands of the Yankees. Or worse, it might even fall to Floyd Bearfield."

Mitchell shook his head. "I've got that thought out. We'll cover all our bets. For precaution we'll string out powder just like you said. We'll keep a man posted out here all the time. If he sees we're losin' our gamble, or the wrong people come after the goods, he can touch off the powder and ride away. If *we* don't get the cache, then nobody does."

David couldn't fault the plan much, as far as it went. "Have you thought out just how we're goin' to get those Yankee wagons?"

"Not yet. But you're a bright lad. I figured maybe me and you could work on it together."

David grimaced. Hell of a note this was . . . rebelling against him, taking his command away, then turning him into a co-conspirator. "You goin' to let me have my gun back?"

Mitchell glanced at Luther Lusk. Lusk said nothing, but his expression made his recommendation for him. Mitchell replied, "Later, Davey, later. With a lot of spilt powder around, there's no use askin' for an accident, is there?"

4

─────

Owen Townsend stood in the open, dusty yard, his good arm folded across his chest, fingers tightly gripping the sleeve that covered the stiff arm. His daughter stood beside him. They watched in grim silence as the Texans who had been left on guard moved out toward the returning men. Homer Gilman and Gene Ivy trotted out to meet them, for they had seen the body tied face-down across the saddle on a led horse. Ivy said in a chilled voice, "It's Pat O'Shea."

There was no need for questions. The absence of Floyd Bearfield was testament enough.

The rest of the Texans gathered as the returning men reached the gate. Some spoke darkly of trailing after Bearfield, but David said nothing. He knew they would realize the futility of it when the first anger had run its course.

Townsend asked the question, though he didn't need to. "Bearfield?"

David nodded.

Townsend said, "I told you you should have killed him when you had the chance. I suppose he got away?"

David nodded again. He swung down from the saddle and looked back at the horse on which they had returned O'Shea. The other Texans listened in silent anger to Otto Hufstedler telling in his broken English what had happened.

"Mister Townsend, we'll bury him here, if it's all right with you. If it's not, we'll take him somewhere else. We wouldn't want to bury him in hostile ground."

Townsend said, "It'll be all right." His daughter started to object, then changed her mind. Townsend continued, "We have a small ranch cemetery up the hill yonder." He pointed to a grove of trees at some distance. "Floyd Bear-field is responsible for some of those graves too."

David studied it a moment, wishing it were Texas. He had seen too many Texans buried, too far from home. "We'd be obliged. I hope you have some spare lumber."

"It's scarce, but there's an extra wagon box in a shed."

David turned, looking for somebody to detail to the job. Noley Mitchell said, "I'll see to it, Davey."

The men carried O'Shea into the house. In a minute, only David remained outside, with Townsend and his daughter. Townsend studied him with questioning eyes. "I expected to see you blow up that whole hill."

"It was my intention. But the men see it differently."

"The men? What have they to say about it? You're the officer in charge."

"I'm the officer, but it would be a shameful abuse of the truth to say I'm in charge."

Townsend grunted in surprise. "What kind of an army do you Texans have, anyway?"

David shrugged. "I don't know. It's the only army I was ever in."

"How you people ever got this far, I'll never understand. An officer commands and men obey. That's the only way an army can be run."

"A regular army, maybe. But there's nothin' regular about an army like ours."

They put O'Shea's crudely built coffin onto Townsend's wagon and carried it up the hill. David looked back every so often toward the north. Sooner or later . . . maybe today, maybe tomorrow, maybe next day . . . a Union detail would come down that long grade with a string of wagons.

The grave had been dug by a couple of Townsend's ranchhands, who waited now, sweaty and begrimed, removing their hats as the wagon pulled up to the site.

David had only the vaguest idea about the differences between Catholic and Protestant. Somebody had told him O'Shea was Catholic and should have a priest for his final services. There was no priest here, and not even a country Baptist preacher. Many a Texan had been buried in this New Mexico soil without benefit of clergy. Sooner or later, some of the ranch Mexicans had told Hernandez, a priest would come through and they would bring him here to give the appropriate rites. Even a *Tejano* deserved a chance at Heaven, they said, because he had been so far from it while here on earth.

Next to Pete Richey, who still lay on a bed down at the ranchhouse, Gene Ivy had seemed the most inclined toward strong religion. David had him read a few appropriate passages from the Townsend family Bible. That was all of the service. David shoveled a little dirt into the grave, then passed the shovel to Noley Mitchell, who in turn passed it on.

Owen and Martha Townsend had come along to honor an enemy who was beyond hurting them. David counted eight boards and crosses in the little cemetery. In the center he saw two which stopped him. One bore the simple inscription: *Amelia Townsend 1819–1861.* The other said: *Patience Townsend Chancellor 1840–1861.*

He glanced at the Townsends. Martha Townsend saw the question and answered before he asked, it. "My mother . . . my sister."

The boards had not yet weathered to the point of being gray. David saw tears well into the girl's eyes, and he had no more questions. He thought now that he understood several things.

The group strung out down the hill, following the empty wagon back toward the adobe buildings. David dropped to the rear. The two Townsends waited and walked along beside him. Townsend asked, "Since you didn't blow up that stuff, what do you intend to do with it?"

"I can't tell you that, Mister Townsend."

"You must be planning to try to take it with you, at least some of it. But how? You couldn't carry much on horseback, and yonder is the only good wagon you'll find on this place."

David hadn't read him the entire letter. Possibly Townsend was unaware of the Yankee wagons. If so, it would be wise to leave him in his ignorance.

Martha Townsend declared, "We just finished burying one of your people. How many more will be killed before you go back where you belong?"

David made no attempt to answer. Frustrated, she declared, "All you people have brought to New Mexico has been death and destruction."

David looked back once at the tree-shaded cemetery on the hill. He could not argue against her statement. "We didn't ask for this war. It was forced on us by people who thought they could walk over us and dictate to us from two thousand miles away. The South has pride, Miss Townsend."

"Is pride worth dying for?"

"A lot of people have thought so."

Owen Townsend said, "I won't argue politics with you, Buckalew. I'm just arguing military realities. You've already lost. All you have left is a lot of political talk. You're a country boy, I take it. What's the largest city you've ever seen?"

"San Antonio, I guess."

"They made a lot of speeches to you there, didn't they?"

"Yes sir, they did."

"I've heard a lot of speeches in *my* time, too. When I was your age I believed most of them. But I'm older now. I find that politics is mostly lies and delusion. They talk to you about glory and duty and honor, all those political people. But at the worst you'll find them to be liars and hypocrites, and at best you'll find them to be damnfool zealots who talk of things they know nothing about. I used to listen to them, but I learned better."

"You don't believe in honor and duty?"

"Real honor, yes, and real duty. But not this empty brassband variety. You remember what I tell you, Buckalew, and if you can stay alive you'll finally come to see I'm right. I've watched too many soldiers over too many years. I've seen them fight their hearts out for what some politician said was duty and honor. And when they had given all there was to give, the politicians would betray them. They would steal the fruits of it. Or they would just throw it away because the public had lost interest, and the average politician won't waste three minutes on something that doesn't help him with the voting public. The soldier does the fighting, but in the end he's at the mercy of the politician. The politician *has* no mercy. He's false, an empty shell. You think the politics of your Confederacy will be any different? The politicians of your government were politicians before there *was* a Confederacy. They'll still be politicians when the Confederacy is gone. To hell with them. Save yourself, son. In your place that's what they would do. It's what they *always* do."

David didn't comprehend half of what Townsend was saying. Probably Townsend was talking about Yankee politics, and maybe he was right. But David was certain government didn't operate that way in Texas; it never had. Sam Houston, in his time, wouldn't have allowed it.

"Mister Townsend, all I know is that we came to New Mexico to do a job. Win or lose, it's our duty to do the best we can. We won't bother you or your people if you'll pledge not to try to interfere with us."

"You know I can't give you such a pledge. You're still the enemy."

David perceived a minor victory. "You *do* believe in duty, after all."

Townsend's mouth pulled down at the corners. "Sometimes we're trapped by our loyalties. We tolerate things we had rather not, because the alternative is disloyalty. Any duty I have is to my country, not to its politicians. The politicians are all back where it's safe and comfortable. I have a duty to our soldiers, because they will suffer if you get away with that ammunition."

That much David could understand. "Then we'll have to watch you and your people. Nobody leaves. Anybody who comes in has to stay in."

"Spoken like a soldier."

That was what David had tried hard to be. "I'll take that as a compliment, Mister Townsend."

"It wasn't meant to be, not altogether. I've been a soldier myself. I find that in many respects soldiers are like sheep. Never ask questions, even when you should. Just believe, and follow orders."

"My people don't always follow *me* too good."

"That's your weakness as a military unit. But it may be your strength as *men*."

Several times during the remainder of the afternoon David walked out to visit with the guard posted on a rise a couple of hundred yards south of the buildings, and east of the small cemetery. David had left his spyglass to be passed from one guard to the next. Each time, he took the glass and looked past the ranch headquarters to the trail which led in from the north. A little before sundown he found the miller, Homer Gilman, on duty. Gilman did not stand at attention as David approached. He gave a civil enough nod, but that was all.

"No sign of anything?" David asked, as he had asked each other sentry.

"Buckalew, there ain't nothin' moved out yonder except jackrabbits, and not many of *them*."

David took the spyglass and trained it on the road. He was divided between a hope the wagons would show up today and a hope that they wouldn't. Every hour the Texans spent here was another hour that some Union command was moving closer to them, or that Floyd Bearfield might use to his advantage. Yet, David had not yet thought out a good plan for taking the wagons away from the Yankees without getting some people killed. Perhaps it would be better if the wagons showed up before such a plan *was* worked out. Then maybe the men would agree to do what he had intended in the first place: blow up the ammunition and go south.

He handed the glass back to the miller, whose face was troubled. Gilman said, "Buckalew, I ain't real sure we can take them wagons."

David grunted. "Neither am I."

He walked back down to the house and entered the room where Pete Richey lay atop a cornshuck mattress on a frame cot. Richey seemed to sense a new presence in the room. He opened his eyes, sighted David and tried to rise up onto one elbow.

David said, "Lie back, Pete. Take all the rest you can."

The boy eased. David seated himself in a chair by the cot. He studied Pete closely but was unable to determine much from his face. It was dark in this thick-walled room. The only large window opened into the patio, and that side was already in the deep shadow of evening. The window to the outside was tiny, just large enough for a defending rifleman to take aim but difficult for someone outside to shoot through.

"Feel any better, Pete?"

"It hurts like hell."

"It'll be better," David said, knowing the words were empty against Richey's pain. But he felt obliged to say *something*.

Pete said, "They tell me we're goin' to capture them Yankee wagons."

His use of the word we *was much too optimistic,* David thought. "Seems like most of the boys want to try."

He caught a tone of fear in the boy's voice. "Sir, if we don't win . . . they'll throw us into a Yankee prison someplace."

"We'll win," David said, thinking himself possibly a liar.

"They'll lock us in some dungeon and let us rot. I don't think I could live if they done that to me."

David became aware that Martha Townsend stood in the doorway. He had no idea how much of it she had heard. He stood up. "Don't you fret about prison, Pete. We'll get you home."

He walked past Martha Townsend. She followed him until they were beyond the boy's hearing. "You don't really intend to try taking him out of here?"

"You heard him. If he stayed it would mean a Yankee prison for him. He'd rather die than face that."

"They wouldn't have to know he's a Texan. We could tell them he's one of our ranch people. They wouldn't doubt us."

David couldn't quite believe. "You'd do that for one of us?"

"Knowing how he was wounded, and where, yes . . . we would. Besides, he's nothing more than a boy. What's he doing here anyway?"

What are any of us doing here? he thought with a clenching of his jaw. He kept looking at the girl, considering what she said. It had a lot of appeal, but he knew he couldn't accept. "I promised we'd get him home."

"Then go now," she said urgently. "Put him in our ranch wagon and go, tonight. Get him out of here before the troops come, and the wagons."

He blinked. She must have heard. "The wagons?"

"Of course, wagons. You crazy Texans are going to try to take over the wagons that come to carry the ammunition and powder away. You'll get yourselves killed, and maybe some of our people too. Please, Buckalew, give it up and go on tonight. Go blow up that cave, if you must, and then get out."

He could not tell her how much he would like to do exactly that. He said, "I'm grateful for what you've done for Pete. You're good folks. I'm sorry that circumstances have set us crossways."

She didn't soften. She said curtly, "I wish circumstances could have set you up a little brighter."

After supper he sought out Owen Townsend. "Mister Townsend, I apologize for the discomfort I'm about to cause you, but I've got to ask that you gather up all your people. You'll all go into the cellar for the night."

Townsend frowned. "It's musty down there. The air's not healthy, especially for the children."

"My men need some sleep. They can't stay up all night and guard you."

It occurred to him that Townsend accepted the situation with a minimum of protest. He expected more argument from Martha Townsend, however, and got it. She pointed out among other things that the cellar was a single room, and there was no way to observe the proprieties if both men and women had to sleep in it. David sympathized but saw no ready answer. He suggested that all the men could face north and all the women face south. Her opinion of that idea was expressed in a word that he could not remember having ever heard a woman use before. She was still talking when the top of her head disappeared down through the opening in the floor.

Noley Mitchell had silently counted off the Townsend ranch people as they went down the ladder.

"You sure that's all of them, Sergeant?" David asked. "We can't afford to miss even one who could slip away and go for help."

"That's all of them, Davey. You need not fret yourself."

David looked down the opening and apologized again to the people there for their discomfort. After letting the heavy door down into place and noting that there was no way to lock it, he pushed a large wooden trunk across the floor and left it sitting squarely atop the door. The strain set his weak arm to aching.

He doubted that anyone standing on the ladder could budge the trunk, pushing upward against its weight. But to be safe he found a couple of clay water pitchers, balanced one atop the other and set them over the corner of the door. If the door lifted as much as a couple of inches, they would tip over. The top one, at least, would be smashed.

"We'll have a couple of the men sleep in here," he said. "The noise will wake them up if anybody messes with that door."

Mitchell appeared at least mildly impressed. "Davey, you're gettin' better. You're liable to make a good officer yet." The smile lasted only a minute. "Now, before we waste any time, I'd best show you what Hufstedler found a while ago."

David followed the sergeant out beyond the adobe wall which surrounded the buildings. The Dutchman leaned on a rifle beside a clump of low brush some distance behind the big house. He straightened as the two men approached him. He pointed silently to the ground.

Hidden by the thorny tangle of low growth was a small wooden door, set almost flush to the ground. David's eyes widened.

"Some of the old houses back home still have these," he said. "Left over from the Indian-raid days."

Mitchell agreed solemnly. "Back where you lived, I don't reckon you ever had the occasion to need one of them get-away tunnels."

"No, but my father says they were handy in his day."

Mitchell's eyes narrowed as he looked toward the house. "In a manner of speakin', them Townsend people are under siege. Come dark they'll try to slip somebody out to go for help."

David looked around for something heavy to put over the door. Not far away was the wagon they had used to haul O'Shea up the hill. He and Mitchell and Hufstedler pulled and pushed it across to the brush by hand and set one of the rear wheels to rest on top of the door. Hufstedler began picking up large rocks and putting them in the wagon bed to add weight. David tried helping him but gave up because of the ache in his arm.

Night was upon them. The air was cool, even crisp, but David found it pleasant. He pulled himself up onto the wagon bed, favoring the arm. He let his legs hang over the empty endgate.

Mitchell left awhile to see that the first shift of sentries were on duty. Presently he came back. "You still here, Davey?"

"Yes. It'll get chilly after a while, but right now the air feels good."

Mitchell squatted on his heels on the ground. The two men sat in silence. David listened for sounds of trace chains and wagons and horses but knew they were unlikely to arrive here in darkness. Even if they were close by, they would probably have camped for the night rather than risk accident to the wagons on a poor trail. No lamps or candles burned anywhere in the house; the place was totally dark.

Mitchell said finally, "I hope you're not still sore, Davey."

"Why should I be sore? All you did was take my command away from me. I'd just as well tear the lieutenant's bars off of my coat."

"Don't do that. You'll need them again, once we get that stuff somewhere that it's useful."

"You know I can file charges on you when we get back to Texas."

"You won't, though, if we're successful. You won't need to if we're not."

"I'll admit that I've been as green as a gourd vine. I've made mistakes since I've been with this outfit. I'd have

made more if you hadn't been along. I'll even admit that
you're the one who should've been the officer over these
men instead of me."

Mitchell nodded. "I'm glad to hear you say that, Davey."

"But the choice wasn't left up to me or you or the men. It
was made by higher authority against the wishes of all of us.
I don't see that you've got a right to go against that."

"Where is that authority now? Do you see it out here
anyplace? Out here we have to make our own authority if
we think it's necessary. And today we decided it was, Davey,
to keep you from throwin' away our chance to win back
some glory for Texas."

David pondered awhile before he asked the question that
had been nagging him. "What about glory for Noley
Mitchell?"

"Well, sure, Davey, there'll be glory in it for all of us if we
can make it work. A little glory wouldn't hurt none of us
when we get home. It wouldn't do no harm to the Buckalew
family, would it? Like father, like son."

"What do *you* need it for, Sergeant? From what they tell
me, you've already had it. They tell me you've been a sheriff for years in your home county. I would imagine you've
already had all the glory a man would ever need."

Mitchell was silent a moment. "You're right about one
thing; I *was* sheriff down there for a long time. But did any
of them tell you why I'm not sheriff any more?"

"I figured you resigned to join the invasion."

"I was already out before that. They voted me out of office, them people back home. They said I'd been in long
enough, that I was gettin' too old for the job, too set in my
ways. They voted in a new man, a young feller not much
older than you are. Green, he was, greener than grass,
takin' over a job I'd worked and sweated and spilled my own
blood for over the years."

"So you joined the volunteers to prove to them they was
wrong?"

"I figured by the time my enlistment was up, and we'd
taken everything clean to the Pacific Ocean, they'd be sick
and tired of that upstart. They'd be tickled to see me come
home. It seemed like for a long time it was workin' out that

way, till Glorieta. Since then there ain't nothin' been right. We've taken one lickin' after another, and we was sneakin' back home with our tails between our legs. Till today. When I seen all that powder and ammunition . . . when I reached out there and touched it and finally realized it was real and not just another wild daydream . . . I could see that I had been given one last chance . . . *we* was given one last chance."

David stared at the outline of him in the darkness. "You were always civil to me, Sergeant, more than most of the others. But I always felt like even you resented me a little, deep down inside. Now I think I know how much. To you, I was that young man back home, all over again, beatin' you out of a place you felt was rightfully yours."

"I tried not to let it show. I'm sorry if it did, because you're not that same feller. With a little more time and experience you've got a chance to be a damned good officer. I hope you can live that long."

"I sure do intend to try."

He became aware of vague rustling noises. Noley Mitchell heard them too, and pushed to his feet. David eased down from the wagon and waited. The noises continued, intermittently, from beneath the wooden door.

The dry wood creaked a little as someone pushed against the door from beneath. It stopped a moment, then a stronger effort was made. The door raised slightly, perhaps an inch, then dropped again. Whoever was down there lacked the strength to lift that wagon and its load of rocks.

David called, "Is that you, Mister Townsend?"

No one answered, but the door no longer moved. David heard a muttering in Spanish, and at least a couple of voices. He said, "Mister Townsend, this is David Buckalew. There's a wagonload of rocks sittin' on top of the door, and I don't believe you folks are goin' to be able to lift it. If I was you, I'd go back and try to get some sleep."

After a long silence Townsend's voice came up, muffled by the small earthen tunnel and the wooden door. "Why didn't you tell us you knew about the opening? You'd have saved us a lot of work."

"I decided you'd take us more seriously if you found out for yourself that we're awake. Maybe you won't take chances that could get somebody hurt. Good night, Mister Townsend."

The voice carried a tone of resignation. "Good night."

At daybreak David scanned the northern horizon for a sign of wagons. Seeing none, he let the Townsend people out of the cellar so they could go about their preparations for breakfast, and whatever else they needed to do. He warned that none were to go beyond the yard.

Soon Luther Lusk, sleepy-eyed from a long tour of guard duty, brought a young Mexican ranchhand into the house at the point of a rifle. "Buckalew," he said gruffly, "you'll want Hernandez to give this *hombre* a lecture on the dangers of not payin' attention. He slipped past the outhouse and was headed over the back fence."

David eyed the Mexican carefully. "You didn't hurt him?"

Lusk lowered the rifle. "Surprised him, is all. He fell off of the fence and landed on his belly instead of his feet. He didn't lose nothin' but his dignity, and most of his breath."

"I don't want to hurt any of these people. They don't know anything about our war."

"They know enough about it to try to help the Yanks."

David had Hernandez ask the Mexican why he tried to get away.

To get word to the Yankee wagon men, he said.

"Why?" David asked. "You don't owe anything to the Yankee soldiers."

The Mexican replied that he owed much to *el patrón*, Owen Townsend.

"He asked you to get word to the wagon people?"

He had asked all of them, the Mexican said, to get away if they could and carry a message north.

David ate his breakfast—what there was of it—nervously and in a hurry, not knowing when a guard posted uptrail would come loping down to the house with news that he had sighted the wagons. But breakfast went by and then the noon meal. In the daylight, David and Mitchell kept only a minimum number on guard, letting as many men as possible rest and catch up on sleep lost to long hours on duty last night, as well as perhaps putting a little on account for the hours they would likely lose in the nights to come.

He made it a point not to interfere more than necessary with the Townsends and their people, though keeping them confined to the house and yard was undeniably a major interference. David looked in occasionally upon Pete Richey. Pete seemed to spend most of his time asleep, or at least half asleep. David supposed this was good; he wasn't sure.

Martha Townsend sat in a straight chair not far from Pete's cot. Her shoulders were slumped. David saw her eyelids gradually close, then come suddenly open as she caught herself. She looked accusingly at David. "Did you ever try to sleep in a closed-up cellar?"

David had no comfort to offer her.

Two hours into the afternoon, the rider he had expected loped into the yard. David stepped out the door in time to see Hufstedler rein up and twist his body half around in the saddle, excitedly pointing back behind him. "They come, *herr leutnant.* Those Yankees, they come."

Noley Mitchell trotted up. "How many, Dutch? How far away?"

"Ten wagons that I count for sure. So much dust, could be more. They are over the hill perhaps two miles coming." In his agitation he was getting the words all mixed up. "There are men riding horses, Noley. A . . what do you call it . . . an escort. They come out in front. They come much sooner than the wagons."

David's mouth had gone dry. He found his voice a little shaky. "Good work, Hufstedler. You go pass the word to the others. They'll all know what's to be done."

Noley Mitchell stared at David Buckalew. "You sure *you* know what's to be done?"

"I know what we've talked about. If it doesn't work . . ."

David went back inside the house. A grim Owen Townsend met him in the front room. Townsend said, "I heard enough to know they're coming. How do you intend to do it without getting my people hurt?"

"We'll try to take those wagons without any fightin'. If we *do* have to fight, you and your people will be out of it. You're all goin' back down in that cellar again. I wish you'd call them together, Mister Townsend."

Townsend's frown deepened. "You really believe you're going to do it, don't you?"

Martha Townsend had lost that tough shell. Her eyes were a little frightened. This was no longer something abstract, a distant possibility they could discuss with detachment. The time was here. Her bluster was gone. She seemed somehow vulnerable for the first time since he had met her, unsure of herself. He told her, "However it goes, it'll be over in a little while. And you'll be all right."

Her eyes met his for a moment, and they held no hostility. Then she was gone down through the trap door. Townsend waited until the last of his ranch people had descended before he went into the cellar. He paused as his shoulders were level with the trap door. "You know I can't wish you victory, Buckalew. But I do hope you come out of this with your life. I'll say this for you Texans: what you lack in intelligence, you make up in nerve."

He went on down, stopping once as another thought struck him. "I suppose you still have the other end of this tunnel blocked?"

"Yes sir."

Townsend sighed and disappeared. David closed the door behind him and slid the trunk over it.

He remembered that he still wore his ruined coat, the only thing left of his original uniform, the only thing that marked him as a Confederate soldier. He draped it across a high-backed chair. It was warm enough outside that he needed no coat. His hat was of a nondescript kind that anybody might wear. It bore nothing of the military except the dust and grime of a long and hard campaign.

David walked into the yard. Luther Lusk followed him. He glanced up toward the hill, where five riders were still a quarter of a mile away. He turned, looking for Noley Mitchell. The sergeant materialized from nowhere. It seemed he was always there when David needed him, and sometimes when David didn't.

"Everything ready, Sergeant?"

"As ready as it'll get." Mitchell's eyes were on the distant riders.

David nodded. His hands were suddenly cold, the palms wet. He ran his right hand over the Colt Dragoon he carried in his belt. Mitchell had given it back to him last night. "Then I'll go out and invite the company in." He glanced at Lusk. "I won't ask you to come with me."

Lusk's eyes seemed to laugh. "But you'd be tickled if I did."

David hated to admit it. "I don't fancy bein' out there all by myself." He started for the gate. Lusk trotted to catch up. The black-bearded frontiersman matched him stride for stride. David walked past the gate six or eight paces so he could clearly be seen. He tried to look relaxed, offering no evident threat to the soldiers who approached. A hundred yards from the gate the five halted. They parleyed a moment, then two came riding on while the other three stood their ground.

"They're suspicious, Davey," Lusk said. It was the first time anyone in the command except Mitchell had called him that. Rather than an affront, he took it now as a sign of progress.

This was the closest David had seen a Union uniform on a live man in some time. One was an officer. The other was a corporal, two big stripes on each of his dusty blue sleeves. The officer's saber bumped against his leg as the horse trotted roughly toward David and Lusk. David had never seen much logic in the saber. In the fights he had seen, a man was likely to be shot before he ever got close enough to use one. The officer, thirty or older, tall and very lean, had several days' stubble on his face. It had been a hard trip, from the weary look of him and the corporal. The Yankees had suffered as much here as the Texans, David thought. Somehow the realization surprised him a little.

He lifted his hand Indian-style as the officer drew rein. The man studied David with a measure of doubt, then let his gaze rove quickly over what he could see of the house and yard.

"Where is Owen Townsend?" the lieutenant demanded.

David had considered posing as Townsend, but he decided some of these men might know him, or at least have been given a description. "He's in the house. He's been taken with a fever."

The lieutenant's eyes narrowed. "And who are *you*?"

"Name is Buckalew." David saw no need to lie about that. There was no reason for a Yankee to recognize the name; he hadn't done anything glorious enough to attract attention. "I'm with Mister Townsend."

"Where are the other troops?"

"Other troops?"

"Another detail was supposed to be ahead of us, under Captain Smith."

"No other troops have come. You sure they're ahead of you?"

"My orders said they would be."

David's heart was hammering. Any minute now, he thought, this officer was going to see through him, and there would be hell to pay. "Some clerk's mistake, more than likely. Would you like to come in and see Mister Townsend?"

The officer frowned at the noncom and took a look back at the three men he had left posted farther out. "Before we move any further, I think that's exactly what I'd better do." He stepped down, handed the reins up to the corporal and waited for David to lead the way.

David said, "I didn't get your name."

"Chancellor. Lieutenant Tom Chancellor. I'm . . . I *was* . . . Mister Townsend's son-in-law."

David shivered, glad he hadn't tried to pass himself or Luther Lusk off as Owen Townsend. That would have been a disaster. "He'll be mighty glad to see you, then." He walked into the house, the lieutenant close behind him. He moved into a second room, well beyond sight or sound of the corporal. David slipped his pistol from its holster and turned, thrusting it toward the officer.

"I'll be obliged if you'll raise your hands."

Chancellor stiffened, his eyes wide. Surprise gave way to anger, and to concern. "Who are you? Where's Mister Townsend?"

"I'm Lieutenant David Buckalew, Second Texas Mounted Rifles. You're my prisoner."

Chancellor had not yet raised his hands. He demanded again, "Where's Mister Townsend? What've you done with him?"

"He's all right." David pointed his chin toward the trunk. "Move that trunk over. You'll find him under there."

Chancellor appeared to know about the door because he shoved the trunk aside and pulled the door up without hesitation. "Mister Townsend," he called anxiously. "Are you down there? Are you all right?"

Martha Townsend's voice cried out, "Is that you, Tom? Tom, this place is surrounded by Texans. They've set a trap for you."

Chancellor glanced back resentfully at David. "I know. I caught both feet in it."

David said, "I'll thank you for your weapons first. Then you can go down and have a reunion." Chancellor grudgingly gave up his pistol and saber, then started down the ladder. As David closed the door and pushed the trunk over it he could hear the anxious exchange between Owen Townsend and Chancellor. He heard Martha say in a breaking voice, "Thank God you're safe."

About that time, Luther Lusk came through the front door with his pistol in the corporal's back. He said, "Here's the next one for you, Davey."

David said sharply, "If you flushed those other three . . ."

"They're still way out yonder. I done this so gentle that they didn't see a thing."

The corporal's face was flushed with chagrin. "I don't understand this. I don't understand this at all."

David studied him a minute. He was not so tall as Chancellor. "I don't believe his uniform will fit you, Lusk."

"It ought to fit *you*, though, Davey."

The next step was somehow to bring in the three riders who waited far beyond the gate. David said to the corporal, "I don't suppose you'd step out there and wave them in?"

The corporal's voice firmed. "No, I would not."

"Then," said David, "I'll need the borry of your uniform."

Lusk watched with interest as David finished putting on the corporal's blue. "Ain't a bad fit," he volunteered. "You'd of made a fair-to-middlin' Yankee if your politics had been different."

David found something a little awry in the fact that even a Yankee corporal had a regular uniform when a Texas lieutenant did not. He said to the corporal, "You can wear my clothes awhile, so you don't have to go down in that cellar in your underwear. Don't worry, I'll be glad to swap back with you in due time."

He stepped out into the yard and into the open gate. The three horsemen still waited a hundred yards farther on. At the distance, he figured, they could not see that he was not the corporal. He waved his hand over his head in a signal for them to come in. He watched until they had ridden part of the distance. He glanced once at the hill. The wagons had not yet appeared. That, he thought, was just as well. He turned back into the yard before the three riders were close enough for a good look at him. He waited just inside the gate, pistol in hand. Lusk crouched on the other side, holding a rifle. They listened to the hoofbeats as the horsemen approached. When the horses stopped, David could tell by the sounds that the men were dismounting. He nodded at Lusk. The two jumped through the open gate, guns pointed. "Just raise those hands to your shoulders," David told the astonished men, "and walk on through the gate."

From out of nowhere came three Texans to take charge of the cavalrymen's horses. The Union soldiers were quickly disarmed and conducted into the house. David studied them and looked at Noley Mitchell. "We need three men who come nearest to fittin' those uniforms."

Luther Lusk was one. Homer Gilman was another. Fermin Hernandez would have been a third, but David reasoned the wagon soldiers might be suspicious of a Mexican in Union uniform; there weren't many. So Otto Hufstedler was chosen as the third.

The three soldiers, dressed in Texas tatters, resentfully went down into the cellar with their predecessors. David walked out front and looked toward the hill. The first wagons were appearing. "All right," he said to Lusk and the others wearing the Yankee uniforms, "we'll ride up there and direct them toward the cave. But we'd better change horses. Those wagon people will recognize these."

The cavalry saddle felt odd to him, though he was riding his own brown horse. He had been using a saddle of his own because Texas had not had funds to equip its soldiers, even if the military goods had been available.

Approaching the strung-out wagons, David counted eleven. One was probably carrying provisions for men and animals. He turned to Luther Lusk. "You've never seen fit to call me by my rank before, but you'd better call me *corporal* this time. They've got discipline in the Yankee Army."

A dark humor showed in Lusk's eyes. "Been kind of demoted, ain't you, Davey, from lieutenant down to corporal?"

Two escort riders were out in advance of the lead wagon. A burly, dusty-faced one wore sergeant's chevrons. He gave a weary half-salute as the Texans approached. "You must be from that advance detail," he said.

Lying had never been countenanced in the Buckalew family, and David had never had much training at it. This had been somewhat of a hindrance to him in his chosen profession, trading horses and mules. But now that he had started, it seemed to come easy. "Yes, we are. Your lieutenant sent us up here with orders to turn the wagons down toward the river. We're goin' to load them right away."

The sergeant frowned. "Why didn't he come himself?"

"They're feedin' him and the others, down at the house."

Resentment quickly flared in the sergeant's round, bewhiskered face. "I could stand some feedin' myself. These men are all tired. They could stand a good night's rest before they commence loading the wagons."

David noticed that the man spoke rapidly and pronounced his words without slurring them or cutting off a "g." The Townsends did the same way. It sounded odd to him, but it set him to worrying that his own manner of speech might give him away. "My captain says he wants the wagons loaded now so we can start in the mornin' and be gone at first light."

The sergeant cursed, every word given the clarity and polish that comes from a long and fond familiarity. "I think I'll go talk to the lieutenant about this."

"My captain outranks your lieutenant," David said.

The sergeant cursed again. "Never saw it to fail. Damned headquarters outfit always takes the best of everything. Any dirty work and sweat job comes along, they always give it to *us*. One of these days I'm going to transfer out of this department and go where the *fighting* is."

David turned away, trying to hide the nervousness and doubt on his face. If he made a wrong move, he thought, the sergeant might find all the fighting he wanted, right here.

He pointed toward the hill where the cave fronted on the river, and he started riding, not looking back or carrying on with the sergeant's argument. Behind, the sergeant groused some more and then sent a private back to carry the word to each of the wagon drivers. "Tell them that damned headquarters bunch has done it to us again," he shouted, making sure David heard.

Luther Lusk winked at David. Quietly he said, "If we keep him mad enough, he won't think about gettin' suspicious."

It was considerably more than a mile down the slope and around the hill to the entrance of the cave. The wagon men seemed in no hurry to finish the trip. David turned a couple of times to look at the afternoon sun. He tried to judge how much daylight time remained, and whether they could get all the goods loaded before dark. All that powder would make it too risky to use torches or lanterns for light.

David and Lusk stayed out well ahead of the wagons, where they would not be drawn into needless conversation that might create suspicion. The sergeant seemed in no mood for anything more than a one-sided harangue anyway. The other two Texans split up along the trail, outriders for the procession.

The entrance to the cave was not visible until David and Lusk went around the hill, the river lying to their left. As they did so, they saw a rider spurring downriver as fast as his horse would run. David and Lusk glanced at each other, not comprehending for a second.

"That was Gene Ivy," Lusk said.

Realization hit David like a mule kick to the stomach. Ivy had been on guard at the cave. Nobody had thought to go tell him what to expect. He had his orders in case the wrong people showed up. And David and Lusk looked like Yankees.

"He's touched off the powder!" Lusk shouted. He dug the spurs into his horse's sides.

David yelled, "No, Lusk! You'll be blown to pieces!"

But Lusk kept riding, spurring at every stride. David held back a moment, trying to think, wondering how far out from the cave Ivy had sparked the powder, wondering how long it would take that racing flame to reach the cave and the explosive cache inside.

David doubted he could help Lusk now, and he owed the man nothing. No, that was wrong. He owed him for being a soldier in the same cause. He owed him for being willing to gamble all he had on a venture he believed in. David spurred after him.

Lusk had a long lead. Ahead, David could see the black smoke racing along the ground, following the trail of powder they had strung out as a precaution. *Hell of a precaution that turned out to be!* he thought, holding his breath as the brown horse raced ahead.

For a few moments he was certain Lusk was going to lose the race. If he did, there wouldn't be enough left of him to bury, and probably not of David, either. But Lusk slid his horse to a stop and was instantly on the ground, down on hands and knees, then scrambling desperately to his feet, shouting God knew what. A few feet ahead of the oncoming flame he began raking sand desperately with his hands, throwing it atop the string of powder, the flame. David could hear him shouting, alternating between curses and prayer. David jumped to the ground and rushed to help him, moving a few feet nearer the cave entrance, his heart in his mouth and choking him; he couldn't have shouted if he had wanted to.

The sparkling, hissing flame sputtered, jumped over and found a spot of powder to burn. Lusk attacked the flame with his bare hands while David leaped down to his aid, kicking sand with his boots. Some if it went into Lusk's eyes, but neither man slowed because of that.

The flame sputtered, flared, sputtered again and went out. Lusk remained where he had quit struggling, on his hands and knees, blinking at the sand, staring at the spot where the fire had burned to a stop. It struck David that the frontiersman's face had gone three shades whiter than normal. Lusk's mouth hung open. Finally one of the man's hands went to his chest, and his face twisted as he struggled for breath.

David realized that his own lungs were afire. He had held his breath too long. And when he took in a long breath the burned powder seemed to sear him. He began coughing, fighting to stop the burning, the constriction of throat and lungs. He dropped to his knees.

For a minute or two he and Lusk knelt there, facing each other, both trying to get a fresh handhold on life.

When finally he had regained his breath Lusk said, "Davey, that was a hell of a lot closer than them Indians."

David only nodded, his chest still heaving.

Lusk said, "If I ever pull a stunt like that again, I hope you'll shoot me."

David nodded again. "That is a promise." Slowly a grin spread across his face, mirrored on Lusk's.

Lusk began pushing to his feet, swaying a little. "Somehow, I wouldn't of thought you'd do it, Davey."

"I wouldn't have thought so either."

Lusk reached out his hand. David took it, and Lusk pulled him to his feet. They began looking for their horses. Both had ended up down near the river. They had stopped and turned back toward the cave, both watching with ears pointed forward, still frightened by the sudden run, the flame and the smoke. They would be hard to catch for a man afoot.

The Yankee sergeant came around the hill and rode up to David and Lusk. The black smoke still clung, fiery to the nostrils. He waved his hand in front of his face as if he thought he could fan the smoke away. "What the hell is going on here? You headquarters idiots been playing with fire?"

Lusk eyed him disgustedly. "There was damn little play in it."

David said, "Confederate. A Confederate tried to touch it off. They're all around us here."

The sergeant looked about quickly, suddenly alert. "Where is he now?"

Lusk grunted. "He left."

David looked downriver, wondering how far Gene Ivy would run before he stopped, and before he began working his way back toward the Townsend headquarters to find out what had become of his comrades. "That is why we need to get those wagons loaded as soon as we can."

The sergeant's face had turned grim. "All right, but don't you think we ought to have some help? How about sending some of your headquarters outfit up here?"

"Most of them are out on patrol," David replied. "They're scoutin' for Confederates, and for Indians."

"Indians too? Goddamn!" the sergeant gritted. He turned and rode back to hurry the wagons.

Lusk grinned again. Those hawkish eyes seemed almost friendly. Gradually David was becoming used to seeing that uncommon expression on the frontiersman's face. "I think we'll get them wagons loaded all right."

David nodded. "Soon's somebody catches our horses for us, how about you ridin' back to the house and seein' how many men can be spared to come out here and help?" It struck him that he hadn't given it as an order; he had said *how about?* "Tell them to remember that they're workin' hands from the Townsend ranch. Anybody says anything about Texas, we've got a battle on our hands."

They lined the wagons up as near the cave entrance as they could. David warned for everybody to hear: "Don't anybody even think about smokin'. One spark in the wrong place and they'll be huntin' for us on the other side of the river. And not findin' us."

The sergeant came up to him and said stiffly, "I'll remind you that you're only a corporal. As the sergeant, I'll give the orders here." He turned toward the men. "No smoking now. That's an order. Do you hear me?"

David had given a good deal of thought to the proper way to load the wagons. He had decided that the powder, being the most explosive, should be concentrated on as few wagons as possible and these kept separated from each other. If one were for some reason set off, distance would help prevent the explosion from starting a chain reaction in the others. He made that suggestion to the Yankee sergeant and added, "That's the way the captain ordered us to do it."

The sergeant growled, "That's the way with those headquarters officers. Full of orders but not of fight. Comes time for the fighting to be done, and the work, who do you suppose they send? *Me*, and my outfit."

David soon found that although he complained with every step he took, the Yankee sergeant had evidently earned his rank with good effort and ability, for he marshaled the wagon men into a very effective work force. Lusk was soon back with several of the Texans, whose status as ranchhands went unquestioned. The sun was just going down as the last keg and the last wooden box were loaded onto the final wagons. The hoops were put in place and the tarpaulin covers spread and tightly secured against the rain that David doubted would ever fall in this drouthy-looking country. He quietly circulated among the Texans as the job was finished, passing orders in a whisper.

As the wagons were strung out around the hill and moved toward the ranch headquarters, the Texans spread themselves strategically on both sides of them. David had feared that sometime during the loading process one of his men would let a careless word fall and betray the whole masquerade, but none did. As the wagons started up the long slope, he began to feel strongly that they were going to get away with it.

Just outside the adobe wall that enclosed the yard, he rode up beside the sergeant and pointed. "We'll circle the wagons here."

The sergeant gave him a look of disdain. "Who the hell says so?" He looked around for signs of other soldiers. "Where is your captain?"

David shrugged. "Out on a scout, maybe. Or eatin' supper."

"I'll be damned glad when *we* get to eat some supper." The sergeant pulled away momentarily and made a motion for the driver of the lead wagon. "We'll circle here."

David waited for him to come back. When he did, David asked, "You have a cook with you?"

"Such as he is," the sergeant said without enthusiasm. "Jones, down on the end, driving the provision wagon. He's a real belly-robber. I hope you've got a decent cook with *your* outfit."

"We've got no cook at all."

"The hell you say! You mean we've got to put up with Jones again? What's the matter with those idiots at headquarters, anyway? Don't they know that men in the field have got to have something decent to eat or they can't keep going?"

The wagons were circled and drawn in tightly, so that the mules which pulled them would be corraled within the circle made by the wagons themselves. No fences or hobbles would be needed. David watched while the mules were unhitched and unharnessed and a ration of corn put out for them.

The sergeant looked toward the house. "I thought sure they would come on out, now that the work is all done. I'll bet they're sitting in there laughing at us. Always the dirty details, that's what *we* get."

David took a long, careful look. As he had ordered earlier, his Texans had made it a point to scatter out so that each stood beside a Union soldier. All were watching David for a sign. Lusk was eyeing him closely, his expression saying, *This is the time*. David reached up with his left hand and removed his hat, bringing it down to waist level. As he did so, he drew his pistol with the right hand and trained it on the sergeant.

The other Texans drew their pistols and covered the Union men. Anger surged into the sergeant's round, bestubbled face. "Now, just what in the hell do you call this?"

David said, "I call it *capture*. You're our prisoners, Sergeant."

The sergeant didn't comprehend. "I always knew you damned headquarters people were crazy . . ."

"We're not from your headquarters. We're from Texas. You're prisoners of the Second Texas Mounted Rifles."

The truth filtered through the sergeant's anger. He sobered. "What about my men? I don't want you hurting my men."

"Just tell them to do what we say and nobody has to be hurt." David motioned toward the house. "You'll go in there single file, hands up. Lusk will show you where. You'll find all your friends down in the cellar, in good shape."

A touch of hope flickered in the sergeant's eyes. "I suppose you've got that headquarters outfit down there too."

"They never got here. They were ambushed by Indians."

The sergeant regretfully shook his head. "That's too bad. Probably had an officer that didn't know anything except shuffling papers. They ought not to be allowed out by themselves."

David held back the cook Jones and a soldier the cook said customarily helped him. The others went down into the cellar. The four whose uniforms had been borrowed were brought back up to change again. David was glad to shed the blue uniform. The color had not suited him, and the fit was none too good.

He walked back outside to view the wagons in the twilight. He looked a moment to the west, where a faint red glow still clung to the clouds above the distant ragged mountaintops. Now that he had time to pause and reflect, he found his knees weak and shaking. He sat on a wagon tongue and stretched his legs out, rubbing them with his hands.

He heard Noley Mitchell's voice behind him. "It'll pass, Davey. The excitement has caught up with you, is all."

David could not quite believe what had happened.

"We did it, Noley. It was impossible, but we did it."

Mitchell stared thoughtfully across the circle of wagons. "The hardest part is still ahead of us."

David hardly heard him. "The hell of it is, it was so easy. I was wrong, Noley. You were right."

A faint smile tugged at Mitchell's mouth. "We'll know about that later. It's a long ways to Texas."

5

The Yankee cook prepared supper in the open yard, his fire built well away from the wagons so that no stray spark could set off a disaster. David considered how best to feed the prisoners; that sergeant's complaint about hunger had been genuine. He decided not to risk letting them come outside to eat. He had a couple of his Texans help Jones move the food indoors and pass it down into the cellar that served as a convenient prison. They took enough for the ranch people as well as the Union soldiers. Then the Texans ate.

David was hungry, but he postponed his meal. He climbed down the ladder and found himself the object of many hostile eyes. In the lanternlight Owen Townsend, his daughter Martha and Lieutenant Tom Chancellor sat together on an old wooden crate, plates in their hands.

David said, "I apologize if the food isn't good. It's the best we could do under the circumstances."

Nobody said anything; they simply stared at him. David cleared his throat. "I apologize to you, too, for havin' to sleep another night in this stuffy cellar. But this'll be the last one. We'll be gettin' started at first light."

Still nobody said anything. He gazed regretfully at the girl a moment. "Miss Townsend, you can sleep upstairs if you like. So can the other women. You'll breathe better up there."

Her voice was cold. "I prefer the society down here."

Chancellor touched her hand. "Martha, I don't believe those Texans would bother you. It *would* be better for you up there."

She looked at David. "Do you think you could trust us women?"

"Yes, I'd trust you."

"Then you'd be wrong. We would take any chance we saw, and somebody would be hurt. So we'll stay down here and ask for no favored treatment."

Tom Chancellor started to say something. Owen Townsend told him, "Best leave her alone, Tom. She's got the same strong will as . . ." He stopped there, the thought bringing him pain. Chancellor nodded and looked down at the floor.

The air *was* stale and dead in here. David gazed at the girl until her sharp eyes cut him. He climbed up the ladder, suppressing a wish to ask her again. An ungiving lot, these Yankees.

On top, he sought out Noley Mitchell. "It might draw some fresh air through if we leave this door open awhile and open up that escape door outside."

Mitchell frowned. "An escape door is made to escape through."

"We can put a double guard on it for now and close it later when the air has had time to clean up."

"Kind of concerned about them Yankees, aren't you?"

"I don't like to see anybody suffer if they don't have to."

Mitchell grunted. "Whatever you say, Davey. You're the officer."

"I thought that honor had been taken away from me."

"Just suspended awhile, you might say. You've got it back."

David thought it was probably unseemly to thank Mitchell for the restoration of something he had had no right to take away in the first place. But he said, "Thanks."

"Now, Davey," Mitchell suggested. "I think you better go get somethin' to eat, then sleep awhile. Tomorrow's a long day."

"That sounds like an order. I thought *I* was the officer here."

"On sufferance is all, Davey. Just on sufferance."

David didn't sleep much. He rolled his blanket on the ground just outside the circle of wagons where he could hear anything that happened. In short, fitful dreams he kept seeing the whole circle of wagons go up in one grand explosion, with himself in the center of it all. Betweentimes he thought he heard every stamp of a mule's hoof, every cry of the night birds, every yipping note from the coyotes which communicated their affections from the hills along the river. Sometime in the early-morning hours he heard a guard's sudden challenge out in the darkness. He sat up quickly, trying to fix the location.

The guard shouted, "You try to run and I'll shoot you."

A familiar voice came from the darkness. "That you, Homer? That really you?"

Gene Ivy had worked up the nerve to come in and try to discover what had happened to his friends. As David threw the blanket back and got to his feet he heard Homer Gilman laugh. "Come on in, kid. Everything's all right."

Ivy was still trembling when David got to him. The young soldier blurted, "I thought the Yankees had gotten all of you. When I seen them Yankee soldiers comin' toward the cave . . ."

David said, "Those Yankee soldiers were us. We forgot to send somebody to tell you." He explained about the capture of the wagons, about Luther Lusk putting out the powder blaze that Ivy had started.

Ivy looked at his feet. "I'm sorry. I guess I almost lost us the whole thing."

"It was our fault. You just followed the orders we gave you. Anyway, we all survived it."

Ivy was hungry and thirsty. Nothing had been left from supper. David decided it wouldn't be more than an hour or so before light began showing in the east, so there was no point in going back to bed; he wouldn't sleep anyway. He went into the house, opened the trap door and called for the Yankee cook to come up and start breakfast. Mitchell and the others saw to it that the mules were fed.

After everyone had had time to eat, and golden streaks were showing through the bank of clouds hanging low over the hills beyond the river, David went down into the cellar. He found himself looking first for Martha Townsend, though his business was not with her. She sat on the large wooden crate with Lieutenant Chancellor.

David took off his hat. "I hope you slept better than I did, Miss Townsend."

"I'd have no idea how you slept, Texas. I did not sleep worth a damn."

Back home he had been taught that good women did not use that sort of language, though he had found in recent years that his teaching had been somewhat exaggerated. "Maybe tonight will be better. We'll be gone from here."

She didn't answer, but her expression indicated she favored that change. David turned to Lieutenant Chancellor. "Lieutenant, I wish you would call up your wagon drivers, please."

Chancellor's eyes were brittle. "You intend to use our own men to take those wagons to your territory?"

"We had sort of figured on it."

Stiffly Chancellor asked, "What if I do not choose to call up the men?"

"You're a prisoner. I don't see where you've got any choice."

"I have a choice. I can sit here and refuse. If I so order my men, they'll refuse to obey you, too."

"This is no time for games."

"I'm not playing any." Chancellor spoke up so everybody in the cellar could hear him. "No man is to step forward. That is an order."

Anger warmed David's face. "I could have you shot."

"You could. I can only gamble that you won't."

David had never been a good poker player. He never could be sure when he was being bluffed. He started to draw his pistol but decided against it. He knew this would be purely bluff on his part. What could he do if Chancellor called that bluff, which he probably would? He stood awkwardly, his stomach churning from the frustration, complicated by the loss of sleep. He tried staring Chancellor down but saw that he couldn't; the man's defiant gaze was as steady as a rock.

David glanced at Martha Townsend and at the old army scout who was her father. Both glowed in triumph.

David turned to the Union soldiers. "You wagon drivers. I want you out here. Now!"

Most of the men were sitting on the dirt floor. They continued to sit there staring at David, challenging him to do
anything about it. David tried to remember which men he
had seen driving the wagons; he hadn't paid that much attention at the time. He recognized one a couple of paces
from him. He stepped over, grabbed the young man by one
arm and attempted to pull him to his feet. The soldier pas-
sively let himself be lifted, but when David eased, the man
promptly sat down again.

David said sharply, "I'm orderin' you to get yourself up."

The soldier shook his head. "Wrong army . . . sir."

Chancellor said, "They're not going, Texas. And if they
don't go, *you* don't go . . . not with the wagons."

David realized that his rising anger might cause him to
make a fool of himself in front of the enemy. He climbed
back up the ladder and found Noley Mitchell at the top,
listening, "Sergeant," he said, "we have trouble."

Mitchell nodded. "I know. But maybe it's a blessin' in
disguise. I been worryin' about how we'd keep all them
Yankee teamsters under control. We've got men enough to
drive the wagons ourselves."

"That doesn't leave us anybody, hardly, for point or outriders."

"We'll get along. We have to."

Jake Calvin had a suggestion. "Let's pull a couple of them
Yankee soldiers out and shoot them. The rest would go."

David's eyes narrowed. "You know we couldn't do that."

"I could."

David called his Texans together and asked how many
had had any experience as teamsters. It did not surprise
him that Luther Lusk had; he appeared to have done a little
of everything. And Fermin Hernandez had been a freighter
on the San Antonio-to-the-border roads for years, though
mostly using ox teams. Virtually everybody had had some
experience handling teams, for they had come from a farm-
ing country. David put Lusk in charge of the wagon opera-
tion, with Hernandez to assist him. They began harnessing
the mules.

They ran into one complication immediately. Lacking
help from the Union teamsters, they didn't know the

mules. Normally each mule had his own place. Some were naturally lead mules, some wheelers, others accustomed to other positions. Hitched out of their normal order and mixed indiscriminately with mules of other teams, they would not perform as easily as they should.

Fermin Hernandez had an idea. He cracked a whip a few times. It was a well-indoctrinated signal, for most of the mules moved into their individual harnessing positions. They found their places and stood there waiting for the harness.

Hernandez grinned. "Every day, Lieutenant, you learn something new."

David blinked. He had seen teamsters do this, but he would never have thought of trying it.

He went into the room where Pete Richey lay on the bed. Pete asked weakly, "We ready to go, Lieutenant?"

"About. How you feelin'?"

"Fine. I'm ready."

David doubted that. Even in the lamplight he could see that Pete was in worse condition than he had appeared yesterday.

"Pete, this is goin' to be a rough trip. We can make room for you in the provision wagon, but it'll jar the guts out of you. You'd be better off if you stayed here."

Pete almost shouted, "No! I don't want to be no Yankee prisoner. You promised you'd take me."

"And I will, if you want it. But it's goin' to be hell for you."

"I want to get back to Texas."

"All right. Somebody'll pick you up directly. Hope you ate some breakfast."

"Drank a little coffee, is all."

"That's not enough. You need your strength."

"I'll do better next time."

David frowned. He wished Pete were doing better *now*.

He needed a few words with Owen Townsend and Lieutenant Chancellor. He descended into the cellar. "I hate to leave you afoot in this Indian country, Mister Townsend. But I'll have to do it unless I have your word that you nor none of these soldiers will trail after us."

Townsend shook his head. "I can't make you a promise like that. It's their job to go after you."

David glanced at Chancellor, hoping the lieutenant would volunteer a promise for the good of them all. But Chancellor sat beside Martha Townsend and said nothing.

"Then," David said, "we'll have to shoot all the horses and mules we don't take with us."

Townsend's jaw dropped, but he regained his composure. "Do what you have to. We'll make you no promises that we don't intend to keep."

Leaving them afoot wouldn't be enough. Foot soldiers could be formidable. "We'll have to take all the guns, too."

Martha Townsend stood up, her eyes wide. "What if Indians come? What can we do without guns?"

"It's not the way I want it, but if I can't have a promise I've got to do it."

Townsend looked at Chancellor, asking with his eyes. Chancellor said, "You can't leave us defenseless, Texas, not in this country. And I can't promise not to come after you. But maybe I could promise to give you some time. How much time do you want?"

David made a quick mental calculation on the probable speed of the wagons. Men afoot could move faster, he knew. "I'll want thirty-six hours. Promise me none of you will start after us before noon tomorrow and I'll leave you your guns."

"Thirty-six hours?" Chancellor jumped to his feet. "I can't agree to that."

"Then we take all the guns, and I leave two men here to keep anybody from comin' up out of this cellar before at least the middle of the afternoon."

Chancellor wrestled with his conscience and grudgingly agreed. "All right. None of us moves against you till tomorrow noon."

Owen Townsend said brittlely, "It's Tom's decision to make, and he's made it. But I'll tell you this, Buckalew: the Army can't let you get those munitions to Confederate territory, to be used in killing our people. They'll be after you afoot if necessary, and I'll be with them. We'll take the wagons away from you if we can. If we can't, we'll blow them up with you in them. You know a bullet or two in the right place could send that whole mess halfway to the moon."

David looked into the old scout's angry eyes and felt ice in the pit of his stomach. Owen Townsend meant every word. And he would do it, for what did he have to lose?

David turned his gaze to Martha Townsend. A thought came unbidden, and at first unwelcome. But it persisted.

They wouldn't be so keen on destroying that wagon train if Townsend *did* have something to lose. He considered a while and saw no alternative. He stepped back to the ladder and called up. "Sergeant Mitchell, would you come down here, please? And bring a man with you." Mitchell and Hufstedler came down the ladder. David directed them to hold their guns on the Union soldiers.

David told the men, "I want all of you to back up yonder." Puzzled, the soldiers complied. Some of Townsend's Mexican ranchhands moved to the old man's side, sensing that he was in trouble. "Back up," David told them. "Back with the soldiers. You too, Mister Townsend, and Lieutenant Chancellor."

Martha started to retreat with them. David caught her arm. "Not you, Miss Townsend. I want you to go up the ladder."

Her father took an angry step forward. Tom Chancellor took two. "Texas, you turn her loose!"

Noley Mitchell thrust his pistol toward them. They stopped.

"Go on up, Miss Townsend," David said, "before somebody gets shot."

She cast one fearful look back toward her father and Chancellor. Then she started up the ladder.

David waited until she was out of sight. "Mister Townsend, this is one thing I didn't want to do, but you've put me in a tight spot. Anything you do against that wagon train, you'll be doin' against *her*."

He started up the ladder, looking back.

Chancellor stepped toward him until David drew his pistol. Chancellor said, "If you think you need a hostage, take me. Leave that girl here."

"She means that much to you, Lieutenant?"

Chancellor glanced back at Townsend. "Yes, she does."

"You think you mean as much to Mister Townsend as his daughter does? You think he would be as reluctant to blow up the wagons if you were with us as if *she* were?"

Chancellor didn't answer.

David shook his head. "You're a soldier. A soldier can always be sacrificed. A daughter can't. Sorry, gentlemen, but she goes with us and you stay here."

Chancellor took a couple more steps. "Texas, if you're any kind of *man* . . ."

David pointed his pistol and stopped him. "She'll be all right," he promised, "if you leave us alone."

Chancellor was coming up the ladder, still arguing, when David dropped the trap door into place, almost hitting the lieutenant's head. David was glad to be out of the cellar, out of the possibility of being forced to shoot the lieutenant. "He has nerve," he admitted.

The girl warned sternly, "And he'll kill you if he ever gets the chance." The look in her eyes indicated that she might try it herself.

For just a moment David indulged in the luxury of looking back on the peace he had left in Hopeful Valley. He found it difficult to comprehend just how he had gotten in a situation where he stirred up so much hatred. It had not been in his nature.

He said, "If there's anything you need to take with you—woman stuff or like that—you better gather it up." He turned to Hufstedler. "You'll drive the provision wagon. She'll be on it with you and Pete Richey."

The wagons were lined up and waiting to move. David asked Noley Mitchell, "How many extra horses are there that we can't take?"

"Just the ranch stock, and one Yankee mule that's lame."

"We'll have to shoot them, then."

Mitchell's face went into deep furrows. He turned regretfully toward the dozen or fifteen animals gathered in a pen. "We shot all those at Bearfield's tradin' post. I'm out of stomach for that job. What if we taken them with us a ways and turned them loose?"

"They'd come home."

Mitchell nodded darkly, seeing that it had to be. "I'll stay behind and do it, then. I'll also keep them folks in that cellar awhile. They won't know when I leave."

"Sorry to give you the meanest job, Noley."

David swung onto his brown horse and sought out Fermin Hernandez. He found the Mexican watching him, a vague resentment in his eyes. David did not understand the resentment.

"Hernandez, you can take the point."

Hernandez' jaw ridged grimly. "I am a good wagon driver, Lieutenant. But I have known you would put me on the point."

"That's been your position all along."

"Why *my* position? If anybody is to be killed, it will be the man out in front. He will be out there by himself. Always before, they put me there because I am a Mexican, and I am not worth as much as the others. You are like them; you do the same."

David was taken by surprise. "That's not true." But he realized it *was* true. He had done it subconsciously, but the reason had been there all along if he had taken time to analyze it.

He sat on the horse and stared uncertainly at the Mexican. A sense of shame washed over him.

"All right, Hernandez, you take a wagon. I'll put somebody else up there." He looked around and spotted Jake Calvin. "Calvin, you'll ride the point."

Calvin blanched. "Me? What for, Buckalew? Why me?"

"Because I'm tellin' you to."

Calvin began arguing that his eyesight was not good enough, that his horse was too slow for an emergency run, that he felt he could be of more use driving a wagon because he knew mules.

David told him impatiently to get the hell up there and follow orders. Calvin went, but he rode along looking back, talking to himself. David turned to Hernandez. "You satisfied now?"

Hernandez did not reply. David said, "I don't think he's one bit better than you."

Hernandez replied grimly, "He is not half as good." He climbed up onto the lead wagon and took a seat. David's jaw tightened. He gave Hernandez the signal to start. He heard the jingling of trace chains, the creak of leather, the crunch of wide-tired wheels turning under a heavy load. He sat on the horse and waited until all the wagons started, the rising sun shining on their left flank. He looked to the east, studying the hills, each range of them a darker blue than the one before it. He rode down the line to the rear wagon, which was bringing along the provisions. Martha Townsend sat on the seat beside Hufstedler. Her eyes were almost hidden beneath the shadow of a slat bonnet, but David saw them cut sharply at him as he reined up.

He asked about Pete Richey's condition. Hufstedler said, "He is not good, *Leutnant,* but what can we do?"

David looked at Martha Townsend. "Anything you can do to help him, I'd sure appreciate it."

She gave him a hard stare but said nothing.

They had traveled perhaps half a mile when David heard the slow, methodical shooting begin behind them. Noley Mitchell was leaving the ranch people and the Yankees afoot. David gritted his teeth. If he ever got back to Hopeful Valley, he would never kill a horse again.

Because they were so short-handed, he kept moving from the front of the train to the rear and back again, serving as a flexible outrider. Homer Gilman rode behind as rear guard. They halted awhile at noon to rest the mules and eat some bread and meat David had had the Yankee cook prepare along with breakfast. He put another man on point to relieve Calvin. He had decided the only fair thing was to rotate the point. Calvin was vastly relieved to be back from that exposed position.

A little after they set out on the trail again, Noley Mitchell caught up with them. He took a long and careful look at the wagons as he worked his way up the line to David.

David asked, "Did you leave everything in good shape back there?"

Mitchell said sadly, "I left it the way we had to. How's everything with the wagons?"

"All right."

"I didn't have to push the horse too hard to catch you. Anybody follows us afoot, he can outpace the wagons."

"They agreed not to come after us till noon tomorrow."

"That was before you took the woman." Mitchell looked behind him apprehensively, as if expecting to see somebody trailing the wagons. "We'd better spend a short night."

David glanced quizzically at him. "Noley, you talked almighty confident yesterday. You don't look that confident now."

"Things always look easier when you're just talkin' about them."

"How much chance do you think we've really got?"

Mitchell shrugged.

David said, "You didn't show me that doubt yesterday."

"You're a horse trader, Davey. Do you ever tell a man all the bad points about a horse you want to sell him?"

"I never tried to sell a man a string of wagons loaded with gunpowder and ammunition, with Yankee soldiers and maybe Indians huntin' for them."

"That takes salesmanship."

"The kind of salesmanship you and Luther Lusk used on me, you could never use in a horse trade. They'd hang you."

"Don't fret over the risk, Davey; think of the benefits. We was comin' home failures, all of us. Now we got a chance to come home as heroes. Your old daddy will be proud of you, button. And them people of mine who voted me out of office, maybe they'll take a second look and decide old Noley Mitchell wasn't so wore out and useless after all."

David's eyes narrowed. "That why you're doin' this, Noley, to try and win an election?"

"Not just an election. I want to win back what I was in the eyes of those people before the rheumatism started, and the hair and the beard went to turnin' gray."

David didn't try to hide a measure of surprised realization. "You're *usin'* this war, Noley."

"Everybody's usin' this war someway. Them professional Yankee soldiers, it's their career. You came to try and win a reputation you never had. I came to win back one I had and lost."

"I came to fight for a cause."

"So did I. So did everybody here, on both sides. But as long as I'm fightin', I'd rather try somethin' big and lose than try somethin' small and settle for it."

In the middle of the afternoon David rode back to the last wagon. Martha Townsend sat slumped and tired beside Hufstedler. Two nights of sleeping—or not sleeping—in that cellar had worn her down. The trailing wagon caught all the dust from the other ten, and she had a fair percentage of that dust on her face despite the slat bonnet.

David said, "Hufstedler, I'd appreciate it if you'd ride my horse a little while and let me take your place on the wagon. I'd like to talk to Miss Townsend."

She gave him no sign of welcome. "I don't believe we have anything to talk about."

Hufstedler pulled the team to a halt and got down. David handed him the reins and climbed up on the wagon. He set the mules to moving. David sat in silence awhile, her antipathy a wall between them. He glanced back beneath the tarp that covered the wagon bows. "How's Pete? You been lookin' in on him regular?"

"He is not doing well. He should have been left at the ranch."

"You know why we couldn't do that."

"I would have liked it much better if *I* could have stayed too."

"I know." David fumbled with the words, taking his time in bringing them out. "I don't guess it counts for much to tell you I'm sorry the way things came out. You wouldn't be here if it wasn't the only way I thought we could bring these wagons through. There was no other way your father would've backed off."

"He may still not back off. He's loyal to his country."

"But he's a father. I'm countin' on him bein' *more* loyal to you."

She was silent awhile. Her face was hidden behind the bonnet, so he had no idea what she was thinking. Finally she asked, "What do you intend to do with me, Texas?"

"You'll be treated like a lady. There's not a man in this outfit that would even think of doin' one thing . . ."

"I know that. That's not what I meant. Supposing you *do* get these wagons through to your own lines—which I doubt—what becomes of me then? Am I a prisoner of war? And if not, how do I get home?"

"I've studied on that. When we get these wagons safely to our side, you'll be free to go back to your own people."

"How? Through this Indian country, alone?"

"I've thought on that too. You'll have an escort home under a flag of truce. If it'll make you feel better, I'll lead that escort myself."

She turned and looked at him, her eyes incredulous. "I can't say it makes me feel better, but it *does* surprise me."

"We haven't always been enemies, Miss Townsend. Till a little while back we were part of the same country. I wouldn't of done you any harm then. I won't see any harm come to you now."

She pondered on that. He sensed the wall coming down a little. "Well," she said presently, her voice a bit less harsh, "I've heard of Texas chivalry. That may be carrying it to an extreme. Even if you ride back here under a flag of truce, you can't be sure our troops will recognize it after what you've done. They may take you prisoner."

That was a possibility he had recognized but had forced himself not to consider, lest it turn him back from what he saw now as a clear personal responsibility. "I'm a horse trader," he said, trying to make light of the risk. "Maybe I can talk them out of it."

"You may do well to talk them out of hanging you."

"Why? I just did what a soldier is supposed to do."

"You put on a Union uniform to carry out your plan. If I know anything about the military code—and I ought to—that makes you eligible to hang as a spy. Didn't you think of that?"

"I didn't even know about it. I never was a soldier before."

"That I can believe." She turned to study him, the hostility gone. "I don't quite figure you out, Texas. Why would you take that risk for me?"

"It's my responsibility. I'm the one takin' you away from home."

That didn't satisfy her, and he knew it. The real truth was that he didn't know why he had made up his mind to this. He suspected it might be because of a vague image that kept coming into his mind, unbidden and at odd times when he hadn't consciously meant for his thoughts to drift in that direction.

He frowned. "You sure you never seen me before, Miss Townsend?"

"I don't remember that I ever did."

"Think back. They said you did some nursin' work in the military hospital in Albuquerque for our side and them both. You sure you didn't help treat me, and put a cool wet cloth on my head when I was in fever?"

"I did that for a lot of men. I don't remember every particular one."

"I remember somebody . . . somebody doin' that for me."

"Do you remember her face?"

"I was too feverish to see clear."

She conceded, "It might've been me, or it could've been somebody else. A lot of women helped in the hospital. Old ones, young ones, all kinds. You don't remember anything about what she looked like?"

"I just remember that she looked like an angel."

"That ought to eliminate me. I've been accused of many things, but being an angel was never one of the charges."

"I *hope* it was you."

"We'll never know, though, will we?"

"If it was you, I owe you for it. If it wasn't you, I owe some other lady that I'll never see again. The only way I can ever repay the debt to her is by doin' somethin' for somebody else. If enough favors get passed around by enough people, maybe everybody comes out even in the end."

"You don't sound like a horse trader. You sound like a preacher."

"I been exposed to some of that, too."

She looked at him, but he found it impossible to read what was behind those blue eyes. At least she didn't seem angry any more. She said, "It's too bad we couldn't have met under better circumstances, Texas. You might be a decent sort if you weren't a Confederate soldier."

"My mother always used to say I was a nice fellow. But of course she knew me before the war."

She laughed. Thinking back, he was sure it was the first time he had heard her do it. She said, "You even have a sense of humor."

"You've got to have a sense of humor down where I come from, else life will drive you crazy. It isn't always an easy country."

"That isn't the way I've heard most *Tejanos* tell it."

He warmed a little, sitting beside her with the hostility gone. He gripped the reins tightly to help fight down a strong impulse to reach over and touch her. To do that, he knew, would destroy whatever good feeling he might finally have attained from her.

He said, "You told me you wished we could've met at another time. I wish we had, too. You suppose that if we had, there's any chance you might've looked at me the way you looked at Lieutenant Chancellor?"

She grew suddenly wary. "I didn't realize I looked any particular way at Tom Chancellor."

"You did."

"He's . . . well, he's part of the family."

"Seems like he thinks a right smart of you."

"He loved my sister. Maybe he sees something of her in me, that's all." She turned and looked him in the eyes, and he saw a wall of sorts come up again. "In any case, Mister Buckalew, that is a personal and private matter that doesn't concern you."

"No, ma'am. I guess I spoke out of my place."

"I believe you did."

Eventually Hufstedler came back and swapped places. David was more than ready. It had become awkward and uncomfortable to sit here beside Martha Townsend after she lapsed back into her stony silence. He had tried a couple of times to start a new conversation in some other direction but had not been able to break through that cool reserve.

David went back to working first one side of the train and then the other, watching for anything that might indicate trouble.

Late in the afternoon Homer Gilman loped up from his assigned position behind the train. David spurred back to meet him, knowing he wouldn't leave his place unless it were important. Gilman reined the horse to a stop, the dust swirling around him.

The tall miller looked agitated. "Lieutenant, I thought them Yankees wasn't to trail after us before tomorrow."

"That was the agreement."

"Well, they've busted it, I expect. There's a man walkin' behind us, gainin' on us from the way it looks."

David tried to see through the dust left hanging by the wagons, but it was hopeless. He frowned. "Just one man? You sure?"

"One is all I can see."

David hesitated, not wanting to leave the wagons but knowing he had to. "All right, let's go see about your Yankee."

Once they had dropped back a hundred yards or so where the dust had either settled or drifted off, he could see the man, possibly half a mile back on the trail. He was out in the midst of a broad, open flat. He was obviously alone. But David looked to the hills on either side, distrusting the obvious. He rode in an easy trot, not rushing into anything. Long before he and Gilman reached the man, David drew the rifle from its scabbard beneath his leg. He laid it across his lap, ready. Gilman watched his action, then did the same.

Even covered with gray dust, the man's clothes were plainly Union blue. David began to suspect the truth before he was near enough to see for sure. For the last two hundred yards, knowing nobody else could be hidden out of sight in this open flat, he touched spurs to the big horse. He held the rifle down to present no threat, but he did not put it away. He stopped just short of Lieutenant Chancellor.

Chancellor carried a rifle in his hand and wore a pistol on his hip. He made no threatening move with either.

David cleared the dust from his throat and spat on the ground. "You made an agreement, Chancellor. And you broke it."

"I made that agreement before you took Martha with you."

"You figured to take her away from us? One man?"

"No. I figured to come along and be with her."

"If I'd wanted you, Chancellor, I'd of taken you the first time you offered. Now you've got a long walk back."

"A long walk, maybe, but not back."

"What do you think you could do for her?"

"Protect her."

"She needs no protection from us, and we'll give her protection from anybody else that comes along. So go back, Chancellor."

"No. I've come a long way. I'm staying."

David stewed, uncertain what move to make next. "Gilman, take his guns."

Gilman stepped down. Chancellor gave up the rifle and pistol without resistance.

David said, "You'll need these for your own protection. We'll give them to you when you turn around and start back."

"I'm going to your wagon train, Buckalew. If you want to stop me, you'll have to shoot me." He waited a minute, watching David's eyes without evident fear. "See, I knew you wouldn't do that. So like it or not, Buckalew, you have another prisoner."

"You'll be one till the war is over."

"That can't amount to much, perhaps two or three months. When they see you Texans retreat from New Mexico they'll know it's hopeless all over the South."

Gilman said, "If you don't want to shoot him, Lieutenant, I expect Jake Calvin would do it for you. It's a specialty of his."

David shook his head. "I'll ask no man to do somethin' I wouldn't do myself."

Chancellor seemed not a bit surprised. "Now that we've settled that question, Buckalew, how about letting me ride double with one of you? It's been a long walk."

David grimaced. "You wasn't invited. I reckon you've *still* got a ways to walk." He turned and started riding away, Homer Gilman beside him. Chancellor seemed resigned. He started walking.

When they had ridden a hundred yards David told Gilman to go on. He turned and rode back, walking the horse, giving Chancellor plenty of time to look at him and wonder.

He reined up and let Chancellor walk the last thirty or forty yards. "You taken an awful chance," David said firmly. "What if Indians had come upon you out there, one man afoot and by himself?"

"Some chances a man has to take."

David was still distrustful. "Does the girl really mean so much to you, or are you thinkin' maybe you'll get lucky and do somethin' to our wagons?"

Chancellor looked him squarely in the eyes. "She means that much to me."

David studied him hard. The man's earnest look made him inclined to believe, but that graveling doubt still lingered. "I've seen prettier women. And she's strong-willed. She can stab you to death with her eyes."

"You, perhaps. Not me. There's another side to her, a side you haven't seen."

David wished he could remember that for certain. "You've taken an awful chance for nothin'. We won't let anything happen to her."

Pain came into Chancellor's eyes. "Someone promised me that once about her sister. I lost *her.*"

David wanted to take him for what he appeared to be. "You promise you won't do anything against our wagons?"

Chancellor deliberated, then shook his head. "I'm still a soldier. No, I won't promise you that."

David cursed again, under his breath. It would be much easier to be tough on a man who wasn't so damned honest. He kicked his left foot out of the stirrup. "Step on up here.

If you're bound and determined to get there anyway, I don't see any gain in makin' you walk."

As they approached the rear wagon David asked, "You bein' an officer and all, I suppose it would violate your dignity to drive a team of mules."

"I've done it before."

"Then you can drive the provision wagon. That's where Miss Townsend is at." He didn't feel he could trust Chancellor on one of the munitions wagons. And this, at least, would free Hufstedler to serve as an outrider.

He rode up beside the wagon and watched for Martha Townsend's expression as she saw Tom Chancellor. She cried out in surprise, "Tom!" For a moment her blue eyes lighted. Then her face changed as realization came that he was a prisoner, just as she was.

David said, "Hufstedler, stop the wagon. You've got a relief driver. You can saddle you a horse."

Hufstedler climbed down with a heavily accented expression of gratitude and stared curiously at the Union officer as Chancellor climbed up on the wheel.

David watched gravely as the two put their arms around one another. He felt a fleeting pang which he knew was jealousy, and realized he had no valid reason for it, or even any right. He started to pull away, for he felt like an intruder. But he had to have his say. "Chancellor, so you understand your place, don't ever forget you're a prisoner of war. You'll find no guns on that wagon, and you'll not go anywhere within reach of any other wagon. You'll stay at the end of the train and keep the same distance as the others. You won't turn off to the right or left, and you won't make any move to get away from here with Miss Townsend. Try any of those things and somebody'll just naturally have to shoot you."

Chancellor nodded. "We understand each other, Buckalew."

"I sure hope you understand *me*, because I think this good woman has already had trouble enough."

It took a long time for word to work its way along the wagons that the Union lieutenant was a prisoner. Most of the men up front had been in no position to see David bring him in. But somehow the word gradually spread, in that mysterious way that news always has in a military organization. One by one, the outriders dropped back to see for themselves.

As David rode by Jake Calvin's wagon, the skinhunter called him. "Hey there, Buckalew!"

David ignored the call the first time. The second time he rode over beside the wagon. "The name is *lieutenant*."

Calvin spat low, streaking tobacco juice across the turning wheel. "Buckalew, I hear you brought that Yankee officer into the outfit."

"He's a prisoner."

"Dangerous, havin' a man like that around, with all this powder and stuff. If I was you, I'd play safe and shoot him."

David nodded. "But you're not me." For which he would ever be grateful to a merciful God. He rode on, leaving Calvin still talking, much dissatisfied.

A while before sundown David loped to the lead and halted the wagons in the center of a wide open flat. Here, he thought, nobody could surprise them. As a precaution, nevertheless, he had the wagons start moving into a circle. He told each driver in succession that they would stop and fix a quick supper, then move on a few more miles before stopping for the night in a dry, fireless camp. The mules had been watered an hour earlier at a natural catch basin that fortuitously had had some water in it. They would be fed a little now while the men awaited supper.

He rode to the last wagon. "Miss Townsend, we're makin' a stop here for supper. There's no man in this outfit that's really much good at cookin'. I was wonderin' . . ."

He had looked back a few times and had seen Martha Townsend and Tom Chancellor in earnest conversation. The sight had always brought a flare of jealousy that he realized was needless. He meant no more to that girl than one of these Yankee mules.

She said, "I don't suppose being a prisoner carries any privileges?"

Chancellor told her, "You don't have to do anything you don't want to."

David said, "That's right, ma'am. You don't have to. But if you eat the men's cookin' a time or two, I think you'll *want* to cook." He made it a point to sound plaintive, and it seemed to work. She said she would see what she could do. Homer Gilman rode up and shoveled a firepit for her at some distance from the wagon circle. Gilman, Chancellor and David lifted from the provision wagon the things she needed for cooking. That done, David climbed back into the wagon for a close look at Pete Richey. At first he thought the young soldier was asleep, and he decided to leave him alone.

Richey opened his eyes. They looked more feverish than before. David felt his forehead and found it almost hot. Richey asked in a husky voice, just above a whisper, "Could I have some water?"

"You betcha." David brought it to him in a dipper and held the boy's head up to help him drink. Slowly Pete took most of the water. What was left, David poured onto a rag which Martha Townsend had been keeping wet and applying periodically to the boy's head.

"Pete," David said, "I'm sorry to be puttin' you through this."

"I could've stayed. Nothin's your fault."

Yesterday David had been hopeful about the boy. But Richey seemed to have lost ground. David lied, "You're goin' to be all right." After his face would betray his doubt, he turned to leave.

Pete called weakly, "Lieutenant!" David stopped. Pete said, straining at it, "They done a lot of talkin' together, that Yankee and that girl."

"Talkin'?"

"Most of it they kept low to where I couldn't hear what they said. I think you better watch them."

David was not surprised. It was only natural that the two would try to figure a means to get away from here. "They'll be watched every minute. There's not much they can do."

"They argued a right smart over somethin'. I heard him say it would be too risky for her, and she said it was worth the gamble. I wish I could tell you what it is. They just wouldn't let me hear."

"I'll do the worryin' about it; you just lay easy and rest while the wagon is still."

He climbed down to the ground and walked out where the fire had been kindled in the shallow pit, downwind from the wagons so no spark would be carried to them. The coffeepot was already on. Martha Townsend was mixing up some water-and-flour bread. David was glad the Yankees had brought that provision wagon along. There was even cured ham in it, and potatoes, At least the men would have something decent to eat on this leg of the trip.

While supper was being prepared, David stood around worrying about the things Pete had told him. He tried to imagine what kind of plot the pair might have worked up. If they intended to run for horses, that was almost certainly doomed to failure. The horses were tied to wagons, and chances were that the Texans could catch the pair before they could ride away. They wouldn't shoot the girl, but they would probably not hesitate to shoot Chancellor out of the saddle, if he ever got that far. Surely Chancellor and the girl had figured this out for themselves.

Maybe they hoped to grab a gun and somehow gain an advantage. It would probably be futile, but they might feel it was worth the effort. David quietly passed the word to the men to hold their distance from the pair and give them no such opportunity.

Through supper he watched, puzzling. When Jake Calvin got too close, David stepped up to remind him of his earlier warning. Calvin said, "I was just hopin' he *would* grab for my gun. I'd be tickled to shoot him."

"I don't want any killin' here," David told him brittlely. "I don't want anybody causin' a reason for one."

Calvin glowered. "I thought killin' was what we went to war for."

Supper finished, the men walked by and dropped their plates, cups and utensils into a pot of water bubbling and boiling over the fire. Tom Chancellor, under David's watchful eye, had brought some fresh wood a few minutes earlier and placed it under the pot to bring the fire back up to a high level. The men began moving back, a few at a time, toward the wagons, ready to move on as soon as David gave the word.

He had just about made up his mind that Martha and Chancellor had either given up a plan for escape or intended to do it later, perhaps during the night. Suddenly, when he had stopped expecting anything, Martha Townsend began running out across the open flat. The move puzzled him for a moment; she had no possible chance of escape that way. A man on a horse could overtake her in a minute.

Nevertheless, she had his attention, and the attention of the men. David realized she was running alone. He turned quickly on his heel, looking for Tom Chancellor. The lieutenant was sprinting toward the wagons, carrying two blazing firebrands he had jerked from beneath the pot.

David had no time to give chase, or even to shout. Chancellor was already more than half the distance to the wagons. David pulled out his pistol, leveled it and started to fire. He let the muzzle dip, for he realized suddenly that a bullet which struck in the wrong place might set off a wagonload of powder. He leveled the pistol again, lower this time, and shot at Chancellor's legs.

The Union lieutenant went down, sprawling, the blazing wood sailing out in front of him. He tried to regain his feet but couldn't stand. He got to one knee, grabbed a brand and hurled it toward the nearest wagon. It fell short. He reached for the other, but Luther Lusk had reached him. Lusk kicked the burning stick away just as Chancellor's fingers had started to close on it.

Martha Townsend stopped running. Only one man, Homer Gilman, had started after her. He stopped too. The girl came back when she saw Chancellor down. She was crying, "Don't shoot him again! Please don't anybody shoot him again!"

She dropped to her knees at his side and threw her arms around him protectively. Her eyes sought out David Buckalew. "Please, Texas. Don't do it."

David realized then that he still had the pistol aimed at Chancellor. He lowered it, for the danger was past.

Not all of it. Jake Calvin had stood paralyzed in those few anxious seconds. Now he walked up with pistol in his hand. "Dammit, Buckalew, I tried to tell you. As long as he's alive there ain't a one of us safe."

He brought the pistol into line with Chancellor's head. Fear leaped into the lieutenant's eyes. The girl screamed.

David shouted, "Put it down, Calvin. You're not goin' to shoot him." As he spoke he brought his own pistol up again, pointing it now at Calvin.

Calvin said, "Girl, you step back or you'll get his blood splattered all over you."

David could see in Calvin's eyes that the hidehunter really intended to do it. "No!" David warned. "I'll kill you!"

Confidently Calvin said, "You wouldn't kill me over no damnyankee." He leaned down, bringing the muzzle of his pistol near Chancellor's head.

"Oh God," David whispered, and he squeezed the trigger. Flame belched from the heavy pistol. Jake Calvin lurched backward under the impact. His pistol went off by reflex, the slug lifting a spray of sand almost at David's feet. The Texan sank to his knees, dropping the pistol. He stared at David in a moment of agonized disbelief, then flopped face forward to the ground. He twitched, and that was all.

David's pistol was frozen in his hand. He could not bring himself to move, even to lower his arm. His nostrils burned from the bite of the black smoke. Tears rushed into his eyes. He found it in him to turn away, closing his eyes in pain at what he had done.

Noley Mitchell gripped his arm worriedly. "You all right, Davey? That bullet didn't ricochet and hit you?"

David found voice, though a broken one. "I'm all right."

Noley waited for David to say more. When David didn't, the sergeant put in, "That Calvin never did have any sense."

David knew, but he asked anyway. "You sure he's dead?"

"He's dead."

David shivered. He found his holster and put the pistol away. He didn't want to turn and look, but he felt compelled. Fortunately, Calvin's face was away from him. David didn't think he could have stood to look into those accusing dead eyes.

He heard Martha sobbing. She was still on her knees, her arms around Chancellor. David took a couple of slow steps toward the pair. "You can get up. Nobody's goin' to kill your man."

His own men were standing around, too numb to move. David tried not to look into their faces, for he was fearful of what he might see.

He brought himself to say, "Somebody better look at Chancellor. See how bad he's hurt."

Nobody seemed in a hurry about it, but Luther Lusk finally knelt and ripped the trousers leg open with his knife. A cupful of blood spilled out. Homer Gilman walked over to help him but didn't appear eager. Lusk gripped the leg and moved it a little. Chancellor's sharp breath reflected the pain. Lusk said, "I believe you missed the bone, Davey."

David looked regretfully at Calvin again. "Yeah, well, patch him up. Get him onto the wagon. We got to move."

Martha Townsend got to her feet. She faced David, the tears still brimming in her eyes.

David said accusingly, "I don't see that you've got anything to cry about. He's still alive. He's goin' to stay alive. That's more than I can say about Jake Calvin."

"We didn't intend it to end like this."

"You'd of blown up the whole train, and like as not yourselves along with the rest of us."

"But how many others would we have saved?"

"It didn't work like you figured. We've got a man dead, and I'm the one who had to kill him. I've got to live with that, if I can."

"I'm sorry."

"Sorry you tried, or sorry it didn't work?" He turned away, toward his horse, then stopped. His voice was cold. "It was for nothin' anyway. The wagon he tried to throw the fire into . . . there wasn't any powder in it."

He told Sergeant Mitchell to see that Calvin's body was placed in one of the wagons. They would bury him tonight, farther on. Right now they needed to make as many miles as they could. He turned in the saddle and watched from some distance as the wounded lieutenant was carried to the provision wagon. He stayed to one side while the train strung out again.

David watched the evening star come out and mentally calculated how many hours it would be until the Yankee troops at the Townsend ranch started after them, if indeed they hadn't broken the agreement and started already. He decided to keep rolling far into the night. There would be time enough to rest men and mules when they had reached other Texas units and safety.

He estimated they had traveled two to perhaps three hours in darkness when the lead wagon stopped. The others had to halt as each drew up close behind the next. David loped to the lead wagon and found Fermin Hernandez standing by his team, afoot. Just ahead, in the darkness, loomed a rough hill.

"What's the matter, Hernandez?"

The Mexican pointed. "Too rough for the dark, Lieutenant. I think maybe I hang the wagon or turn it over."

Reluctantly David had to agree. "Pull them back a little, then, and start a circle. We'll stop here." He stood by while the wagons began moving into position. As the last one made its move, he rode in beside it. He said to Martha Townsend, "You and Chanceller will get down easy and be placed under guard inside the circle. There'll be no fire here. We'll bury Calvin, then we'll get some rest while we can."

Sadly she said, "I'm sorry to tell you, but you'll need to dig two graves. Pete Richey died in his sleep."

David clenched his fist and turned quickly away. He drove the fist futilely at the pommel of the saddle until the pain made him stop.

6

~~~~~

At first light the wagons were strung out again. It was not proper to call this a trail, for there was none. If any wagon had ever passed this way before, it had left no mark.

David hung back a little, his shoulders hunched. The two graves had been left unmarked because it was said that Indians sometimes dug them up and mutilated the bodies. He had no idea if this was true, but he had chosen not to run a risk. The wagons had deliberately been driven over the spot to obscure it. When the Texans left, no one would ever know that two of their number had remained here, forever. David doubted that he could find the exact place again himself, once he rode away from it.

He took off his hat. "We tried, Pete. We tried hard to get you back to Texas."

He rode on after the others. He imagined he could feel Martha Townsend's eyes upon him as he passed the trail wagon, but he made it a point not to look. He rode with his head down, leaving something of himself back there in those graves.

He rode up on a hill where he could see a long way in three directions. In particular he looked behind him. He saw nothing. But he could feel it gnawing at him; back there, somewhere, those Yankees were coming. He could feel them.

He took a position about even with the middle of the train and held it except for occasionally riding out to a prominence for a long look. Sometime about midmorning Noley Mitchell fell in beside him. The sergeant moved along in silence awhile, framing with care the thing he wanted to say.

"It's tough enough to kill an enemy," he said quietly. "It's tougher to kill your own kind. But Jake Calvin wasn't really ever one of us. He was just along."

"I keep askin' myself if I should've done it. I traded his life for a Yankee. If I had to do it over . . ."

"You'd have to do the same. Hell, Davey, there's not a man in the outfit that thinks you done wrong. It took guts to try what Chancellor did. If he'd managed to hit powder like he hoped, he wouldn't have had one chance in ten of gettin' away fast enough. He knew that. If he *is* a Yankee, he's a man. Jake Calvin never was."

David took a long time to digest that. He didn't say anything.

Mitchell made a lengthy study and came up with no answers. "I hope you're feelin' better," he said, probing.

"No, but I thank you for comin' and tellin' me, just the same."

They halted briefly at noon to fix coffee, eat a little leftover bread, fry up some ham and give the mules time to "blow." David saw to the men and the wagons before he took time to go in and get something to eat. He walked to the fire and poured some coffee. As he looked up, he found Martha Townsend staring at him. Their eyes met; he could not avoid her.

He asked, "How's Chancellor?"

"A lot better than he would be if you were a good shot."

"I *am* a good shot. Otherwise I'd of killed him."

"You mean you weren't trying to?"

"I wouldn't of shot Jake Calvin if I had wanted to kill your man."

She frowned. "He's not *my* man, the way you say it." She looked down. "I've said some hard things to you, Texas. I won't say that I didn't mean every one of them at the time. But I wish I could take them back."

"I wish I could bring back Jake Calvin, too. But I can't."

Her eyes commanded attention. "We had a duty, Texas, just as you have. We had to make a try. It's still a war, and we're still on opposite sides."

David could understand that. He had pleaded the same reasons just yesterday. Some of the bitterness lifted. "I hope you won't try again."

"Tom is in no condition to."

"But *you* are. It's bad enough havin' Jake on my conscience. For God's sake don't make me go through life rememberin' that I had to shoot a woman too."

She considered. "I won't. We've made our try."

The first sign of the trouble came an hour or so later. He saw a horseman at some distance on the left flank, toward the river. He halted, extended the spyglass and took a look. The rider was an Indian, moving at an easy walk paralleling the train. David's throat tightened. He scanned the hills as far as he could see, looking for more. He saw only the one.

Homer Gilman came loping up shortly, pointing in the same direction. David nodded. "I've already seen him. It's an Indian."

"What kind?"

"I don't know. All I know about Indians is that none of them seem to like us."

An hour or so later, one of the Texans on a wagon began gesturing at David, trying to get his attention. From his wagon seat he pointed off to the right. A quarter mile to the west, or a little more, was another Indian.

Noley Mitchell rode back to fall in beside David. "You've put the glass on them, I suppose?"

About that time the Indian to the west rode up on a hill and dismounted. David could see a mirror flashing.

Mitchell growled. "If it was a telegraph wire, we could cut it."

"Maybe we could anyway. A few of us could rush him and kill him."

Mitchell shook his head. "Too late. Killin' one now might be like killin' one ant out of a whole anthill. Anyway, there might be a bunch of them waitin' in ambush out yonder, hopin' we'll try that very thing."

David decided it was a good time to make use of Mitchell's experience in fighting Indians, an experience David himself had never had. "What do we do, then?"

"Keep on doin' what we're doin' now, just travel. There may not be many of them after all. If not, they're probably just hangin' on, hopin' for a chance to grab a few horses or mules. We'd best keep the wagons tight together."

The men were already taking care of that. The gap between the wagons had narrowed almost to nothing. Everybody on the train had seen the Indians.

David dropped back to the last wagon, where Martha
Townsend rode beside Hufstedler. A grim-faced Tom Chancellor watched out the back. "Buckalew," he said, "under
the circumstances, don't you think we ought to have some
guns on this wagon?"

"They haven't made any hostile move yet. *You* have. You
feel strong enough to be drivin' this wagon?"

"I guess so."

"Good. We can use Hufstedler on horseback."

Martha Townsend's lips were tight. "Those Indians, Texas
. . . what do you think they're going to do?"

"They're *your* Indians, Miss Townsend. I expect you
know more about them than I do."

There was no question of moving these wagons after dark.
David had heard somewhere that Indians would not attack
at night, but he had no faith in that story. He reasoned that
if he were an Indian he would fight anytime and anywhere
that he had a strong advantage, and darkness would certainly be an advantage to those out yonder if they intended
to hit moving wagons.

At sundown, reaching a reasonably flat and open stretch
of country where the bushes were scattered and short,
David ordered the wagons drawn into a tight circle. The
mules were unharnessed. They and the horses were turned
loose for feed and water inside the formation. From the
standpoint of Indian danger, he thought, it would have been
safer to build the cookfire inside, too. But that would be too
risky from the standpoint of the gunpowder. They dug the
firepit away from the wagons but near enough that they
could retreat in a hurry. Nobody lost any motion in getting
supper started; Martha Townsend had more help than she
needed.

David had never yet seen more than the two Indians.
These had continued to ride along at a respectful distance,
out of effective range, keeping up with the wagons but making no threatening move toward them. David wished he

could tell himself that these two were all. But he sensed that they had company, somewhere yonder out of sight.

By dusk everybody had finished eating. The firepit had been covered with dirt to prevent flying sparks. With the night came a chill. David hunched his shoulders and wished the tattered gray coat were heavier. He had half the men out on guard duty. The other half, theoretically, were to sleep so they could stand guard later in the night. He doubted that anyone would shut his eyes.

He walked to the place where Martha Townsend and Tom Chancellor huddled together, each wrapped in a blanket. David looked at the girl, but he asked Chancellor, "How's the leg?"

"It hurts." He hadn't been able to walk on it. Somebody had had to support him and help him hop along. Well, he wouldn't be trying to run away, or running to destroy a wagon.

Chancellor said, "If it comes to a fight, you *will* give us guns, won't you?"

"Only if you give me a promise."

"You have it."

Well, that was a change for the better, anyway. David turned to the girl. "Miss Townsend, I'm sorry we've brought you to this. But if you hadn't been with us I expect we'd be surrounded by Yankees now instead of by Indians."

"Would that make any difference?"

"Not from our standpoint, I suppose. We don't seem to have any friends in this country, red or white."

Out in the night, a small fire began to flicker. David watched it and shivered from the chill. Well, some Indian was getting warm. In a few minutes another fire started, and another and another. In a little while a dozen or fifteen small fires burned at intervals all the way around the train.

Noley Mitchell walked around the circle, checking the guard. He stopped where David leaned against a big wagon wheel, watching.

David asked, "You figure they'll come against us tonight?"

"They might, but more likely they'll wait for daylight, to where they can see what they're doin'."

"They probably don't know what's on the wagons. If they've got guns, and they come in shootin', a bullet is apt to send this whole thing up in one big puff of smoke."

Mitchell grunted. "That's been my thinkin' too."

"The main danger is the powder, Noley. What if we take everybody we can spare and put them onto shovels? We can bury it."

"Good idea, button. I wisht I'd thought of it."

Nobody was sleeping anyway, or likely to sleep much tonight. They got onto the shovels. The men would work awhile, then swap places with the guards. The digging went on all night. Before daybreak they had dug a long trench. They began unloading the powder wagons, putting the kegs into the hole. When they had done with it, they threw a goodly amount of dirt over the kegs, packing it down tightly as they went. They piled cases of rifles and bar lead on top of and around the hole, setting up an additional barrier to stop bullets or turn them.

David worked with the rest of the men, so long as his bad arm let him. Those Indians wouldn't give a damn whether he was an officer or not. When the job was done he leaned against a wheel and looked out into the night, cold now from the sweat in his clothes. He could see color starting to break in the east. He saw fires beginning to flare up at intervals around the wagons.

The fires had worried him all night. For lack of any personal experience he tried to put himself in the Indians' place. If he intended to attack somebody, he doubted that he would make a big show of his presence for hours beforehand. He would be more likely to try to move in secrecy. The Indians had seemed to be making a show of their numbers, as if trying to scare the wagon people.

It occurred to David that they might be hoping the Texans, in their fear, would saddle up and ride off in the night, leaving the wagons behind. There might be more fires out there than Indians. Many a fight had been won on bluff.

But as daylight came that hope drifted away. The red sun lifted over the mountains and shone down full upon a rough circle of horsemen scattered all around the train, most of them two to three hundred yards away, waiting. David held his breath until his lungs started to ache, and then he took a rushing gasp.

Somebody—he thought it was Lusk—demanded, "My God—did you ever see so damned many Indians?"

David tried to count, but he could not see all those on the opposite side of the train. He guessed there were seventy or eighty, maybe as many as a hundred.

"What do you suppose they are?" he asked Noley Mitchell, not that it made any particular difference.

Martha Townsend gave the answer in a tight, unnatural voice. "Comanches. Maybe some Kiowa. They range into this country sometimes."

Luther Lusk called from his post. "If they rush us, Noley, what's our chances?"

Mitchell shook his head. "Damned poor."

The men had all armed themselves with rifles from the Yankee wagons, and each had plenty of extra cartridges within arm's length. David pointed to a broken case of rifles. "Miss Townsend, you'd better grab you one, and get one for Chancellor. Take ammunition, too. This time we're all on one side."

He shivered from the morning chill as he watched the Indians, wondering when they were going to come. His mind drifted back to another morning not long ago, when he and his men had waited behind hastily piled rocks on a mountain farther north, expecting any minute to be over-run. He felt that same cold knot of dread in his stomach, that same cold sweat making the rifle slippery in his hands.

He looked longingly toward the south and wondered at the treachery of fate. They had come a long way, but now it appeared this was to be the end of it. They would never get back to Texas.

Otto Hufstedler called, *"Leutnant!"* He pointed to the northwest. David spun, raising the rifle instinctively to his shoulder, expecting to see the Indians moving against them. He lowered the rifle and blinked, trying to clear the haze that his anxiety had put in the way. He saw a single rider coming toward him, carrying a big piece of white cloth tied to the muzzle of a rifle. He kept waving the rifle so the cloth would not be overlooked.

Quartering in, the man was hard to see in any detail at first. The nearer he came, the more evident it was that he was not an Indian.

Somehow David knew who he would be before he saw the face.

Floyd Bearfield stopped his horse fifty yards short of the wagons. He called out, "Is Buckalew in charge of the train?"

David hesitated, then answered, "I am. State your business."

"The rifle is empty. I have no cartridges with me. I want to come and parley with you."

"I don't see what we've got to parley over."

"You don't? Then you must be blind. Take another look at all my friends out here."

Martha Townsend's voice came from behind David. It was edged with hate. "Call him in, Buckalew. Call him in closer and I'll kill him!"

He saw the hatred in her eyes. He had no doubt whatever that she would do it. "Noley, you'd best relieve Miss Townsend of that rifle."

She said incredulously, "You're not actually going to talk to him? He'll lie to you. He'll make any promise to get what he wants, and then he'll kill you."

"He's in a good shape to kill us anyway. I'd as soon talk first." He turned to Mitchell. "Noley, I'll walk out a little ways and meet him. I don't want him gettin' close enough to see that we buried the powder."

"He's liable to get you out yonder and kill you."

"He's in easy rifle range. I doubt he'll try anything that would get him killed."

As David walked out to meet him, Bearfield moved cautiously closer. David had left his rifle behind, but he wore his pistol. Bearfield saw it. "I see you're armed, Buckalew. I've already told you I'm not."

"I know you *told* me. Now, what is it that you want?"

Bearfield's bewhiskered face was grim. He hadn't shaved in days. He looked as if he hadn't slept, either. "Well sir,

Buckalew, the situation is somewhat changed from the last time we talked. This time I have a few good cards in my hand."

"You don't have the whole deck, though."

For some reason David felt a strange confidence now that he stood face to face with this man. He found his voice coming through with a strength he couldn't have explained. Perhaps it was the knowledge that at this moment he still had the upper hand over Bearfield on a personal level. Regardless of the eventual consequences, it was in his power to kill Bearfield anytime he took the notion.

It was a struggle to beat down that notion.

Bearfield said, "I think it would be to the advantage of both of us to make a trade."

"What have you got to offer?"

"Life, instead of death."

"In return for what?"

"You know I know what you have in the wagons."

"And you know what it's for. Our troops need it."

"I'm not greedy, Buckalew. I realize you're a patriot, and I respect that. All I'm asking for is a division. Give me half the wagons and you can go on your way. You'll still have the other half, and surely you Texans can wage a good fight with just half of what is in that train."

"What happens to the half that you take? Who will *you* use it against?"

"That needn't concern you. Your enemies are my enemies too."

"But some of your enemies are my friends, my own people. You'll trade that stuff to *your* friends out there, and they'll use it on raids down into *my* country to bring back stolen goods to trade to you. I'd rather blow it all up right here."

Bearfield's brow knitted. "And kill all your own men, and yourself in the process? Surely patriotism doesn't have to carry you that far. Nobody has to die. I am trying to reach an accommodation with you so that everybody can live."

David saw that he had one strong point of leverage, Bearfield's craving for the goods on those wagons, and his fear that they could all be lost in one suicidal gesture by the

Texans. "You can't afford to attack us, Bearfield. One misplaced bullet from your people and it all goes up. Or, if I see we're about to be overrun, *I'll* blow it up. Either way, you lose what you've come for."

Bearfield's sharp eyes cut into David's; he tried to determine if David was bluffing. That unexpected strength let David stand his ground and meet Bearfield's steady gaze without flinching. Bearfield broke first. He looked away a minute, clenching his teeth so that his cheekbones seemed to push out.

"You may not be totally aware of your predicament, Buckalew. You have more than just my friends and me to worry about." He pointed north. "Just a little way from here is a force of Union troops with Owen Townsend. They're afoot, or they would already be upon you. They went into camp last night about three miles back. By now they're on the move again."

David tried not to let his surprise show. Assuming Bearfield was telling the truth, the Yankees had not abided by their original agreement. He could easily understand why they might feel that his taking Martha Townsend would negate all promises. After Chancellor had left, they had probably talked it over among themselves and decided to move.

Bearfield said, "So you see, Buckalew, if you do not give the wagons to me, the Union troops will be on you before long. Even if my friends and I pulled back, you couldn't get much farther. At least we offer to let you keep half the wagons. The Union will make no such offer."

David said nothing.

Bearfield started again. "You wouldn't have to worry about the soldiers at all. Make a deal with us and we'll take that problem off of your hands. You'll have a clear path all the way back to Texas."

"You'd kill those Yankees?"

"They're my enemies as well as yours."

A picture came to him, bringing back the chill of the night just past. David saw those Union troops he had found strung out in death through that canyon to the north. He shuddered. "I don't know as I'd want them to die that way."

"What difference does it make to you how they die? You Texans have been killing them for months, and being killed by them."

"But that was war."

"What do you think *this* is? It's been war here for two hundred years. Those people out there started first against the Spanish, and then against the Mexicans, and later against the Americans. This is their kind of war. Let them fight it for you."

David was tempted, but only for a minute. That bloody picture kept coming back, that scene in the canyon. He wondered how many more such bloody scenes would result in other places, including Texas, if he gave up even half of this wagon train.

He said, "I reckon we'll take our chances with the Yankees, and we'll take our chances with you. Don't you forget that it'll take just one shot to blow the whole thing plumb across the river. Now you'd better go back out yonder to your friends."

Bearfield instinctively brought his rifle around at David, then caught himself and looked with concern toward the wagons. He said tightly, "Buckalew, I'm offering you a chance to live. You're a fool."

"Not a blind fool, Bearfield. If we gave you half the wagons, how long would it be before you came after us to get the other half? You're too greedy a dog to settle for half a bone."

Bearfield seemed disposed to argue. David drew his pistol. "Maybe you're unarmed and maybe you're not. But I *am* armed, and I'm tellin' you to move."

Cursing, Bearfield rode away. David walked hurriedly back toward the wagons, looking over his shoulder most of the way.

Noley Mitchell met him, rifle in his arm. "He wanted the wagons?"

"Half of them. He said if we'd give him half the wagons he'd let us go."

Martha Townsend's eyes were anxious. "You didn't deal with him?"

"No. He wants them all. You can bet he wouldn't let us get far without givin' up the others."

Mitchell said, "There ain't much we can do, surrounded like we are. We can't move."

"They don't know we've buried the powder. Bearfield's afraid to rush us because he doesn't want the wagons blown up."

Martha Townsend said, "You had the advantage over him. Why didn't you make him a prisoner? We could have used him as a hostage against the Indians."

"He was under a flag of truce."

Her temper flared. "At a time like this, you worry about formalities?"

It hadn't even occurred to David to do it. Such a move would have been against his instincts.

"So now we just wait here," she said, exasperated. "For what?"

"For a break."

Mitchell said soberly, "I don't know what."

David pointed north. "If Bearfield wasn't lyin', those Yankee soldiers aren't far behind us, afoot." He looked at the girl.

Hope flared in her eyes, until a grim realization set in. "How many men?"

"However many we left in that cellar, I expect."

"Against this many Indians? They'll be killed."

He hadn't seen real fear in Martha Townsend's eyes until now. She demanded, "Did he say anything about my father? Is he with them?"

David hadn't intended to tell her, but he couldn't lie. "Bearfield said he was."

Martha Townsend turned away. She sank to her knees beside Tom Chancellor. He reached out and pulled her to him, letting her cry against his shoulder. Chancellor looked up at David. "You should have killed Bearfield when you had the chance, Buckalew. He's destroyed half of the Townsend family already. Now I suppose he'll get the rest of it."

David knew the Townsends' hatred of Bearfield was too deep to be based on general principles. "It's time somebody told me what he's done to the Townsends."

The telling was painful to Chancellor. His face twisted as he talked. "I was stationed in Albuquerque. My wife—Martha's sister—was going to have our baby. Her mother came up from the ranch and persuaded me to let her take Patience back home to have it. There was sickness in Albuquerque then, and I was afraid for Patience and the baby. Owen Townsend had sent wagons for supplies, and a force of men for guards. Mrs. Townsend assured me Patience would be safe. And I thought she would be, too, safer than in Albuquerque.

"But on the way home, Indians hit the wagons. They came so fast, and so many of them, that nobody had a chance. My wife . . . Mrs. Townsend . . . everybody was killed except a couple of men on the trail wagon. They got cut off and made it to shelter in some rocks. The Indians didn't seem to feel it was worthwhile rooting them out. When it was over, Bearfield and some of his Comanchero traders came and drove the wagons away. They were in league with the Indians."

That cold chill came back to David. He looked at Chancellor, and he looked at the girl. He understood much now.

They had a scare once. Fifteen to twenty Indians gathered, parleyed awhile, then suddenly came riding. As they neared the wagons they dropped down behind their horses, only a little of a leg and an arm showing. For a moment David thought Bearfield was risking the wagons. The Indians let fly a volley of arrows. Most of them fell short. No shots were fired except by the Texans. One horse went down, and then another. The two Indians were on their feet instantly to be picked up and carried off. So far as David could see, none were hurt.

Mitchell said, "Just lettin' us know their intentions are serious."

David nodded. "And lettin' us know they think they can take us without usin' guns."

He thought about it a little and ordered one keg of powder dug up. He used an ax to chop a hole in one end. To nobody in particular he said, "I told him we'd blow up the whole thing rather than let it fall into his hands. It's time to show him *our* intentions are serious."

He carried the keg beyond the wagons, looked around to be sure no Indians were near enough to overrun him, then started in a straight line in the direction where he considered Bearfield to be. He let the powder string out thinly as he walked. Fifty yards from the circle he stopped and set the keg down. A couple of Indians were riding toward him, but they were a long way off. Even in a walk, he could beat them to the wagons.

He did not intend for them to see him run. He walked, though briskly. Where he had started stringing powder, he stopped, knelt and fired his pistol into it. The powder sputtered into flame. It flared, the flame racing outward in a trail of black smoke. He glanced at the Indians. They were still coming. He took the last three strides that put him inside the wagon circle.

When the flame reached the half-empty keg it exploded, sending fragments of wood flying high beneath a cloud of black smoke. One of the Indians' horses broke into frenzied pitching. He threw his rider, who sailed through the air with arms and legs flailing. David turned his face away instinctively to avoid being hit by any falling debris. It was too far out; none of it reached the wagons.

"That," he said, "will give him somethin' to worry about. He wants these goods worse than he wants us."

He watched the Indian horse run away, the Indian chasing after it in total futility.

No more Indians came against the wagons, but they remained out there, spread in a rough circle.

It occurred to David that he was hungry. They had never even made coffee this morning. "We'd just as well fix breakfast. I doubt as anybody is goin' anywhere for a while."

They did their cooking much nearer the wagon circle this time, for the powder seemed safe enough. Martha Townsend went about her work tight-lipped and shaken. David told her, "They ain't got us, ma'am. Not by a long ways."

"We have a trump card," she said. "But my father's out there somewhere without anything. They'll kill him, Buckalew. You know they'll likely kill them all."

He wanted to say something to comfort her. "There's quite a few soldiers with him. Good soldiers, I'd expect."

"They're afoot."

"Don't the Army sometimes send infantry out against the Indians?"

"They do, but the man on horseback has all the advantage."

He gave up the effort and moved away from her. But he kept watching her from the corner of his eye, feeling guilt for having brought her into this trap, no matter how good his reasons had seemed.

Mentally he began figuring distances and walking times, wondering just where Owen Townsend and those Yankees would be by now.

Presently he began to see movement among the Indians. He tensed, bringing up his rifle. But the movement was lateral, not toward the wagons. He saw that a major number of the Indians were heading north, taking their time.

"They ain't leavin' us?" Luther Lusk exclaimed, incredulous.

Noley Mitchell shook his head. "Don't get your hopes up." He walked to David, took a quick glance toward the girl, and said in a voice she couldn't hear, "I expect Bearfield was tellin' you the truth about them Yankees."

David nodded. "Bearfield figures they'd blow us all up rather than let us get back to our lines with the powder. He can't afford to have them do that."

"They wouldn't do it with *her* here."

"Bearfield probably doesn't know she's with us." He went for his spyglass, pulling it open. He studied the departing Indians, then tried to get some idea how many were remaining behind. These were only a scattered few, a token remnant, probably staying to be sure the wagons didn't move.

Mitchell said, "They'll wipe them Yankees out. It may take them a while, but they'll do it."

"The thought pleasure you any, Noley?"

"I can't say as it does. And I can't see where it'll help us in the long run. The Indians'll be back for us in due time."

"But the Yankees will thin them some. And while the big bunch is gone, maybe we can thin these others ourselves."

Mitchell stared at him, his mouth open.

David said, "Ask for volunteers. Half of us will saddle up horses and get ready. The rest will stay to guard the wagons."

"Which half am I with?"

"The half that stays here."

"It'd be a real favor to me, Davey, if you'd let me go. It'd mean a lot to me when I get back home."

"But it's my place to go. You're second in command. You've got to stay and take over in case I don't get back."

Most of the Texans wanted to volunteer, so David hand-picked them, trying to leave as strong and dependable a group with the wagons as he took with him. They saddled their horses quietly, hoping not to get any particular attention from the Indians who waited out there, one small group on the east, another four hundred yards to the west.

The main body of Indians left a trail of dust as they moved north. The seven men were ready and waiting impatiently for David to give the word. He steadied the spyglass on a wagon and watched the half-dozen Indians to the west. The riders would be coming at them out of the sun.

Luther Lusk said, "What we waitin' for, Davey?"

"For distraction. The closer we get to them before they see us, the better chance we'll have." He waited, looking up from the glass to rest his eye, then going back to it to be sure nothing had changed.

Gunfire erupted somewhere to the north. He saw the waiting Indians turn away from the wagons, listening. Most of them were afoot, their horses quietly grazing nearby. The warriors were wanting in on the fight. *Well*, David thought, *here's a good time to give them one of their own.*

"All right. Let's go."

They led their horses out between the wagons and swung up with rifles in their hands. David didn't bother to look behind him. He knew the others were coming. He spurred the big brown horse into a hard lope across the flat, down into a shallow ravine and up again. So far as he could tell, the Indians were so intent on what was going on over the rise they hadn't noticed the Texans yet.

One of them saw. He loosed an arrow so quickly David hardly saw him draw it out of the quiver. The range was too long. The Indian sprang for his horse. The rest followed his example.

David fired a quick, poorly aimed shot toward the Indian horses. He knew he was unlikely to hit one, but he hoped to startle them and make them run. Luther Lusk did likewise. The Indian horses began throwing their heads and tails up and running, frightened. Two of the Indians grabbed theirs and swung onto their backs, but the others were left afoot.

"Get low!" David shouted.

He needn't have said it, for the men were already as low across their horses' necks as they could get. The rifles began firing. David saw one Indian go down, and another. He saw the arrows flying at him. He felt the brown horse break stride as one glanced off of his chest, opening a shallow wound.

In moments they overran the foot Indians. The fire was murderous for a few seconds, until not an Indian remained on his feet. The two on horseback had slowed to try to defend their friends, but they were too late. Luther Lusk slid his horse to a stop, jumped to the ground, took careful aim and brought one of the horsemen down. The other rode off.

David didn't have to say anything. He gave a signal and all the men wheeled, spurring back toward the wagons. He looked around to be sure that no one had faltered, no one was hit. Fermin Hernandez' horse stumbled and went down. David reined around. He kicked his left foot out of the stirrup so Hernandez could use it and mount behind him. Hernandez dropped off when they reached safety. He stared at David with surprise and wonder. The Texans paused only a minute at the wagons while David stepped down to check the brown horse's wound. He found it was superficial. He looked through the glass at the Indians to the east. They had moved in closer, confused, unable to tell just what was happening. They couldn't be surprised like the others, but at least they were nearer.

"All right," David said, "let's get them." Hernandez had to stay behind, for there was no time to catch a fresh horse.

David spurred out and heard the rest of the men pounding along beside and directly behind him. The seven or

ight Indians came riding to meet them, stringing their
ows. This time the Texans' tactics were different. Taking a
ue from Luther Lusk on the other run, David stopped the
rown horse suddenly, jumped to the ground, dropped to
ne knee and took aim. Through the billow of black smoke
e saw an Indian fall.

The other Texans did as David had done. They brought
own two horses and three more Indians. The other Indians
ame on, two more falling in the next volley. The rest, seeing
ney were almost alone, reined their horses around and
ent running. The Texans fired after them. They brought
own one more horse, but the remaining Indians got away.

David looked on either side to be sure none of his men
ere hurt. This time they had never allowed the Indians
ithin effective arrow range. "All right, we've ripped them
ome. Let's get back to the wagons."

Lusk said regretfully. "I wisht Bearfield had been
mongst them."

They took their time riding back, for there was no imme-
iate danger that David could see. He kept looking toward
ne north, wondering if the sound of the shooting might
ring reinforcements. But he saw nothing. They were too
usy down there to have heard or seen what happened
ere.

From the north came a ragged pattern of fire, heavy at
itervals, stretching out and almost stopping at others.

Noley Mitchell walked out to meet them. "Looks like you
one right good."

"We whittled the odds a little." David looked around him
ith a pride he hadn't felt in this outfit before.

"Sounds like them Yankees down there are puttin' up a
ood fight. You been listenin' any?"

"Been kind of busy, Noley."

"Sounds to me like they're movin' closer. Probably tryin'
o get to some kind of cover and form a redoubt."

Afoot, David led the hard-breathing horse in between the
vagons. He saw Martha Townsend looking anxiously north-
vard, listening to the firing. She gave the Texans little
otice as they came back from their skirmishing.

He said to his men, "Keep the horses saddled. An[y] chance we get, we'll do it again."

She heard his voice and turned. "Do you hear that?" sh[e] demanded, tilting her head back toward the sound of th[e] guns.

"I hear it. They're makin' a good account of themselves[.]"

"But they can't win."

He knew that. He wouldn't tell her so.

Her voice was struggling not to break. "My father's o[ut] there."

"I'm sorry, ma'am."

He loosened the girth to let the horse breathe easier, an[d] he tied the brown to a wheel. He checked the wound agai[n;] it didn't amount to much. He took out the spyglass an[d] made a long study of the ground to the east, south and wes[t.]

It occurred to him that they could reload the powde[r] wagons and move out of here while the Indians were bus[y] elsewhere. The sudden sortie had left them no effective op[position] position out there. But he considered a little and gave u[p] the idea. They would only face it somewhere else a fe[w] miles farther on. This was as good a place as any to see th[e] thing through.

The men stood around in silence, their faces grave a[s] they listened to the sporadic firing. David wished he d[id] not keep thinking of that other time, back north, but th[e] awful image kept flashing across his mind. He decide[d] Mitchell had been right about the shooting moving neare[r;] the Yankees hadn't yet let themselves be nailed down.

· Martha Townsend shouted, "Look!"

The urgency in her voice made David turn quickly on h[is] heel. He thought he could see movement again, up whe[re] the main mass of Indians had disappeared. He moved to th[e] north end of the wagon circle and braced his spyglass acro[ss] an endgate. He thought at first he was having trouble brin[g]ing the image into focus, but he realized that what he sa[w] was dust. Some Indians were riding back and forth. The[n,] to his surprise, he glimpsed men on the ground, movin[g.]

"Those Yankees!" he exclaimed. "They're still a-walki[n,'] fightin' their way along."

Noley Mitchell rushed to his side, squinting but unable to make out much with his naked eyes. David handed him the glass. Mitchell grunted. "By George, they're a gamey bunch. They just keep on a-comin'."

Tom Chancellor had dragged himself along across the ground. He pulled up on a wagon wheel and shouted, "Let me see! Let me see!"

Mitchell handed him the glass. Chancellor found the action and swore under his breath.

David demanded, "How many do you see?"

"It's hard to tell. A dozen at least, maybe more. They're keeping the Indians at a distance. They're putting up a good fight."

David frowned. They couldn't have much ammunition left, judging by the shooting, and remembering the amount he had left them at the ranch.

Martha Townsend moved close to Chancellor. "Tom, is my father among them? Can you see him?"

"I can't tell. There's so much dust . . ." He lowered the glass, his face grave. "They're trying so hard . . . but you know they can't make it. There's no way they can do it."

Martha Townsend turned to David. Desperation was in her eyes. "Texas, you could help them."

"Ma'am, they're the enemy."

"Right now there's only one enemy."

"They've come here to stop us from gettin' through with these wagons."

"Bearfield has stopped you already. You're going nowhere with these wagons any more, don't you know that?"

David turned away, his face twisting bitterly. "They didn't have to come after us. It's their fight, not ours."

"It'll be yours again, once they've been beaten. Bearfield isn't going to let you move out of here with these wagons. He'll be back for you. You'll need all the help you can get." She grabbed his shoulder and tried to turn him around to face her. "Buckalew, you can help them, and then they'll help you!"

He didn't answer. She cried, "Buckalew, for God's sake . . ." Her voice lifted at the end, and broke.

David still hadn't looked at her. But he looked at Noley Mitchell, at Luther Lusk, at Homer Gilman and Otto Hufstedler.

"What do you all think?"

Mitchell nodded grimly. "I think we could do it."

David looked at Lusk. If Mitchell and Lusk were for it, the rest would follow. "Luther?"

Lusk was torn. He looked regretfully at the wagons, as if mentally giving them up. "Hell yes, let's go."

They saddled the rest of the horses, as far as the saddles would go. They put bridles on some of the mules and tied the reins to ropes so they could be led. The extra horses were also tied to ropes. David quickly picked three men to lead the horses and mules. The rest would form around them in a protective wedge.

Five men would stay here. This time Noley Mitchell insisted that he get to go. Luther Lusk was left in charge at the wagons. The rest of the men led their horses outside and mounted up. David made sure everybody was ready. The animals fidgeted and stomped, sensing the excitement.

David said to all the men, "We may be lucky. Busy as they are, the Indians may not see us at first. We'll do like we did last time . . . we'll ride in fast, pick up the men and ride out again as fast as we can. Anybody falls, it may be impossible to pick him up. We've got to save as many as we can and get the hell away. Everybody set?"

Noley Mitchell nodded. David didn't wait for the rest. He spurred out, hitting a hard lope.

The Yankees were half a mile out now, he judged. He leaned over the brown's neck, trying for all the speed he could get, hoping the men weren't strung out badly behind him. He took no time to look. Ahead he could see the Indians riding in wide circles around the beleaguered Union men. If they had seen the Texans coming they gave no sign of it; their attention was devoted to the men on foot.

For the first time it occurred to David that the Yankees might mistake the Texans for more Indians and start shooting at them. That, he thought, would be a hell of a thing to happen after all the risk his men were taking. It was too late now to reconsider, or to change anything.

The ground flew beneath him. The big brown's long strides reached out and gathered it in. The morning wind bit his face and burned his eyes until they watered, making it more difficult to see what lay ahead of him.

The Indians had seen them. The nearest were rushing out to meet them. David shouted, "Don't let them get close." He fired his rifle before he was in good range, hoping he might hit near enough to slow them down. He couldn't take any real aim from the back of a running horse, no matter how close he might have been.

The Texans all started firing except the ones in the center of the broad wedge, leading the extra horses and mules. David saw one Indian horse go down, but he didn't know if it was wounded or if it had stumbled. Any shot that hit under these conditions had to be purely accidental.

Ahead of them the Indian circle wavered, then broke. Inside it, the Yankees knelt, firing rapidly. The Union men were a hundred yards away, then fifty. Then the Texans were among them, swinging the horses and mules around. David's blood was racing. He didn't try for any kind of count. He thought he glimpsed Owen Townsend, but there was no time for making sure.

"Up quick!" he shouted. "Everybody onto a horse or a mule!"

He didn't have to repeat it. A couple of men, wounded, were helped on. Others jumped up behind them.

A wave of a dozen or so Indians made a desperate charge. Arrows started coming in. David heard the scream of a mule. "Cut it loose," he shouted, "and let's get out of here!"

He fired the rifle at the nearest of the Indians and spurred back into a run again, south toward the wagons. This time he looked back once. He saw the Yankees all up except one, who lay on the ground. They wouldn't have time to help him. They had to move fast, to save as many as they could.

Now, closing on both sides, came the main body of the Indians, fully alarmed, fully aware that the Yankees they thought they had trapped were about to be swept away from them. David fired as rapidly as he could poke cartridges into the rifle. When an Indian came close and he missed him, he whipped out his pistol and fired that, so near he thought the warrior must certainly be powder-burned. The Indian veered away, lurching to one side.

The wind bit David's eyes again. He spurred, listening to the hoofs pounding beside and behind him.

Just ahead now were the wagons. Luther Lusk had pushed one of them out of line to make an opening the men could ride through. David reined off to one side and began pulling up, letting the main body of men pass him by. Back in the heavy dust he saw two men and a horse on the ground. The horse was kicking. David could not tell who had fallen, Texan or Yankee, and knew there was no time to go back. A dozen Indians swept by the fallen men, swinging their warclubs. A couple jumped down. Whoever the men were, they were beyond help.

Arrows whispered past David. He marveled that he had not been struck. Then, suddenly, he was. He felt a jarring impact. Fire cut through his hip. He grabbed at the pommel to keep from falling. He cried out and held on. He had to stay in the saddle; nobody could help if he fell. He dropped the rifle. He saw the men gallop through the opening between the wagons. The brown carried him in that direction, sweeping past two Indians who tried to club David. David leaned over the horse's neck and knew he had entered the circle. He was dimly aware of men hurriedly pushing the wagon back into place, plugging the hole.

The brown carried him into the other horses in a blind rush and lost his footing. He went down on his side, kicking. Instinctively, the breath half knocked out of him, David crawled away. He narrowly missed being trampled by other horses and mules. Someone grabbed him beneath the arms and dragged him. Blinking away the haze, he saw Fermin Hernandez.

Hernandez brought him up against the wheel of a wagon. David could hear the firing as the men, Yankee and Texan, hurried together to hurl back the Indian rush. Somebody fetched a blanket and spread it. Hernandez eased David onto it.

David wheezed, "Much obliged, Fermin." He had never called the Mexican by his first name.

Hernandez said, "It is all even again, Lieutenant."

David tried to sit up, but the strain made the arrowhead cut deeper. He gasped and dropped back onto his side. He could see that the shaft had been broken when he fell, but part of it was still in his hip. He reached to touch it and found his hand warm and sticky with blood.

The firing let up. David kept closing his eyes, then opening them, trying to clear the blur. He saw Luther Lusk standing over him, looking down anxiously. "Luther, did we lose anybody?"

Reluctantly Lusk said, "One, Davey."

David kept looking around. "Where's Noley Mitchell? I want to see Noley Mitchell."

Grimly Lusk said, "He's the one, Davey."

David groaned.

He heard Lusk call, "Somebody help me. We got to take care of the lieutenant before he bleeds to death."

Lusk slit David's trousers from the waistband down past the arrow. Martha Townsend said, "Here, I'll do the rest of it." He could feel her careful hands stanching the flow of blood with a cloth, then she was pouring something over the wound that burned like the fires of hell.

Someone said, "We ought to be able to pull that arrow straight out." Martha Townsend replied, "The head of it might stay in. Be patient. We'll get it out, all in one piece."

Men held David while Martha cut around the arrowhead with a sharp blade. He tried to hold still, but the blade was agony. He could not help himself.

Then the arrow was out. He felt the blood flowing warm, cleansing the wound. Martha let it flow a moment, then dropped a handful of flour to clot and stop it.

The worst was over. David watched through a reddish haze of pain as she applied a folded cloth to the wound, held it a little, let up, then pressed again.

His voice sounded unnatural to him. "Just like it was in Albuquerque."

He could see a faint hint of a smile cross her face. "You never could remember for sure whether that was me or not."

"I want to believe that it was. And I'll always remember that it was you this time." He tried to look around but couldn't make out any faces. "Did your father . . ."

She nodded. "He's here. He's all right."

"How many of your people did we get back with?"

"Ten, I think. I haven't had time to really count."

"Ten. Well, at least we've got you outnumbered."

"It doesn't make any difference. Right now, everybody here is the same."

He became aware that the firing had stopped. He tried to turn his head to see beyond the wagon, but the wheel and a corner of the blanket were in his way. Martha said, "They've pulled back. Talking it over, I suppose. They've suffered a lot."

Someone was standing just beyond David's feet, throwing a shadow over him. David blinked and recognized Owen Townsend. Townsend said, "Buckalew, I see my daughter has finally gotten to use a knife on you. If she had done it any earlier she would probably have used it a lot higher up."

David supposed that was meant in a humorous vein, but he was not capable of appreciating humor now.

Townsend said, "I can't forget that we wouldn't be out here at all if it hadn't been for you. But I thank you for pulling us out of the untenable position they had us in."

David considered his answer before he made it. "I can't apologize for what we did. We had a job to do."

Townsend nodded, gripping his bad arm, which seemed to be paining him. "Each of us does his duty as he sees it."

Another man stopped beside Townsend. He was the burly sergeant David had hoodwinked to get control of the wagons. He frowned down at David, taking his measure. "Texas, I had made up my mind that if I ever caught up with you, I was going to challenge you to a duel. Would you be interested now?"

"I don't believe so," David said.

"I thought not. Since I owe you my hair, I guess it would be a little awkward anyway. But I will admit that you look good there, on your back."

David wasn't sure whether to take the sergeant seriously or not. He decided this was probably the nearest the man could come to saying thanks. He replied, "You're welcome," and hoped it fit. If it didn't, the hell with it. He wasn't feeling up to worrying about it anyway.

Some of the Texas men began gathering around to see about him, now that the Indians had eased their pressure. David tried to sit up. Martha warned, "You've just now quit bleeding. You'll start it again if you don't hold still."

It hurt so much that he quit trying for the time being. He said, "I reckon I'll do my travelin' in a wagon for a while."

Martha replied, "Those people out yonder . . . they're not going to let you leave here in *any* wagon. As long as they want these munitions, and you have them, none of us are going anyplace."

He heard a curse from the end of the wagon. He knew Luther Lusk's voice.

"That son of a bitch! He's comin' in again with another white flag."

David asked, "Bearfield?"

"Yes, him and some Indian. They're comin' in together, wavin' that flag. I'll get some of the boys, and when he gets in range . . ."

David knew the temptation. He had felt it before. But he said, "No, Luther, it's still a flag of truce. We'd just as well hear him out."

"You know what he wants."

"I know, and he's not goin' to get it."

"Then let's just kill him and see what happens."

He heard the voice call from beyond the wagons. "Buckalew!"

David pondered about it. When the voice called again, he said, "Luther, Fermin . . . would you all help me up?"

Martha protested. David said, "I reckon I've got to get up sometime." He had to choke down a cry of pain when they got hold of his arms and pulled him onto his feet. He tried to put weight on the leg but couldn't. He was nauseous for a moment. If they hadn't been holding him he would have fallen on his face.

But his head cleared in a minute. The pain subsided to a level he decided he would have to tolerate. "Take me out there a little ways."

He put his arms around the two men's shoulders. He couldn't help much; they simply had to lift him enough that his feet cleared the ground and they could carry him.

He had them take him out twenty yards. He didn't want Bearfield any nearer the wagons, where he might see that they had the powder buried and protected. That would invite rifle fire against the wagons. He felt Bearfield's eyes burning at him as the Comanchero rode cautiously forward, not trusting the men who aimed their rifles at him from behind the wagon beds and the heavy wheels. If he made one treacherous move, they would cut him to pieces, and he knew it.

Bearfield said with some satisfaction, "Well, Buckalew, you don't look quite as healthy as you did when I last talked with you."

"I'm still here, though."

"Even assuming you live to get back to Texas, you'll be lucky if they don't shoot you for treason, rescuing a detail of Union soldiers. You have aided and abetted an enemy."

"Enemies is one thing I've had a-plenty of out here."

"You're a fool, Buckalew. You don't think those Yankees will ever allow you to take that ammunition train to Texas now, do you?"

David didn't answer. Bearfield said, "I offered you a good deal. I was going to take care of your *real* enemies for you, and leave you with half the wagons besides. Now you've cost us a great deal, and so my price has gone up."

"Your price?"

"You can't go anywhere so long as we don't want you to. You're in a trap. Give us your wagons, and we'll give you your lives."

"That's no kind of a trade."

"It's *my* trade. Leave now and you can all leave here alive. We'll get the wagons. Stay, and none of you will leave alive. We'll *still* get the wagons."

Luther Lusk gritted, "Say the word, Davey, and I'll shoot the son of a bitch."

Bearfield was plainly apprehensive, but he did not give ground. David shook his head. "No, we won't kill him. Not yet."

Bearfield appraised the wagons. "I know what you're thinking; you believe you're safe because we can't afford to shoot into the wagons and risk blowing them up. But I'll bet you've never seen a real rain of arrows, have you, Buckalew? If I turned these people loose to do it their way, there wouldn't be a man, a horse or a mule left alive." He jabbed his finger at David. "One way or another, we'll have those wagons. The only difference is whether we do it with you alive, or all of you dead. For my part, I can't say I really care very much." He began backing the horse slowly. "Talk it over with the rest of them. Make up your minds. I'll give you an hour to draw back from the wagons. After that, you're dead!"

He pulled his horse around and began riding away in a walk, giving everybody a good view of his back, almost as if daring someone to shoot him. David imagined the man was probably in a cold sweat, dreading that somebody actually would. But he was also making a show of his bravery for the benefit of the Indians.

Lusk said, "It'd sure be easy to do it right now." He had one hand on the butt of his pistol.

David said, "Get me back to the wagons. Call everybody over for a conference. We're goin' to talk this out."

They gathered around him . . . Lusk, Hernandez, Hufstedler, Gilman, Gene Ivy and the rest. In a quiet, strained voice David told them of Bearfield's ultimatum.

Lusk said heatedly, "I'd rather give it back to the Yankees than to him." The others nodded agreement.

David said, "But we can't afford to give it to the Yankees, even if *they* could get away from here with it. We can't give it away, and we can't move it. So what do we do with it?"

Lusk looked at the others, then back to David. A heavy sadness was in his face. "I guess we'll have to do what you wanted to do in the first place, Davey, what me and Noley wouldn't let you do. We'll have to blow it up. Then nobody gets it."

Gene Ivy's eyes widened. "But how do we do that? We'll blow ourselves up with it."

David felt Luther Lusk's sadness. He said, "Good men have died for what's in these wagons. If we blow it up, they died for nothin'."

Lusk shook his head, then raised it a little in a show of pride. "Not for nothin'. They *tried*, Noley and the rest of them. We *all* tried. We can look the whole world in the eye and tell them we gave it the best we had."

David looked them over thoughtfully, each in his own turn. He had realized for some time now that it might come to this, in the end. "Is everybody agreed, then? If not, this is the time to speak."

Gene Ivy asked again, more anxiously this time, "But how can we do it without blowin' ourselves up too?"

"Easy," David told him. "We won't be here."

Ivy nodded, then realized he didn't understand a bit of it. But David let his questions go. "Luther, Fermin . . . you all reckon you can lift me onto my horse and tie me onto the saddle?"

Lusk frowned. "It'll be hell on you."

"It's hell anyway, lyin', standin' or a-horseback. First, help me over to those Yankees. We'll tell them what we've decided."

As Lusk and Hernandez carried him, the Union people began gathering. Martha Townsend began telling him he had better lie down, but he told her he probably wouldn't by lying down again for a right smart of a spell. He told them all, "We're goin' to leave the wagons."

Owen Townsend immediately protested, "You can't leave these goods to that butcher!"

David grimaced, the hip throbbing as if someone were driving a red-hot spike into it. "He's not goin' to get them. Neither are you, and neither are we. Ain't *nobody* gettin' these wagons."

Martha said tightly, "You're going to blow them up?"

When he nodded, he thought he saw her smile. She said huskily, "Thank God."

Somebody had helped Tom Chancellor hobble to join the group. When the Union sergeant protested that the wagons were government property, Chancellor said, "Let it go, Sergeant. Too many people have died already."

Martha said, "And more would die, no matter who got the wagons . . . the Union, the Texans or the Indians. It's time to end it, and this is as good a place as any."

David saw no argument, except perhaps in the eyes of the Union sergeant. He was muttering something about those "stupid incompetents back at headquarters," and how they would never understand or condone this. "They won't even believe what's happened here. I hope you don't leave it up to me to write the report, Lieutenant. I'll lie, that's what I'll do."

"I'll make the report," Chancellor promised.

David ordered the powder kegs dug up and at least one placed in every wagon, with a hole knocked in it. The men knocked holes in other kegs and strung powder around and through all the wagons. After that, each one caught a horse or a mule. They used the saddles as far as they would go, and the rest would have to ride bareback. They took all the provisions they could carry, tying them behind the saddles.

Several of the Texans lifted David onto his brown horse. He hovered on the brink of unconsciousness for a moment. He knew he was bleeding afresh. Perhaps there would be an opportunity later to stop it and make a new bandage. If not, it probably wouldn't matter anyway, for chances were he would be dead. Luther Lusk looked up anxiously at him. "Goin' to make it, Davey?"

"What choice have I got?"

Lusk and some of the others took up the remaining few kegs of powder and stove in the ends. One of the wagons was pushed a few feet so they would all have room to pass out of the wagon circle. Martha Townsend, Tom Chancellor and a few others were riding. Most of the rest walked, leading their horses and mules, making a shield so no one watching from afar could see what Lusk was up to.

They began moving out in a walk, in single and double file at first, then grouping just beyond the wagons to make a tight company. David held to the pommel of the saddle as the brown walked. Every step brought a stab of pain. He turned to look back. Lusk was walking along, spilling a thin trail of powder. When Lusk's keg was empty, Homer Gilman took up where he had left off. When Gilman's was gone, one of the Yankee wagon men continued the job.

David tried to watch the Indians, but his vision was blurred. He couldn't bring them into focus. His heart was beating like a hammer. He had little faith in Bearfield's promise that they would be freed. If Bearfield had any inkling of what they were doing, he would set the Indians loose on them instantly.

David remembered the ravine he had ridden across on the first sortie. *That*, he thought, *would be a good place to stop*. If they had to make a stand, it would provide at least some cover.

They reached the ravine. David made a signal for the others to ride into it. It was not as deep as he had thought. Standing in it, afoot, Owen Townsend showed from his chest upward. The Union sergeant and a couple of his men stepped forward to help David down, but he demurred.

"It hurts more to get up and down than it does to stay up."

He watched Otto Hufstedler empty the last powder from the last keg, twenty yards out from the ravine. They were now a hundred yards or a little more from the circle of wagons.

Luther Lusk pointed. "Looky yonder, Davey. They're startin' in."

David's teeth clenched tightly. He tried to make out Bearfield but couldn't be sure. He took the spyglass from its case and extended it, but he was too weak to hold it steady. "Here, Luther, take this thing."

Lusk held it to his eye a minute. "Yep, yonder's Bearfield, lopin' in. He's more eager than the rest of them, looks like."

David could see a blurry movement, though he could tell little about the man. "Luther," he said, "this is somethin' I'd rather do myself. But since I can't, I'm goin' to ask you to do it. Anytime you think it's right."

Lusk reached up and grasped David's hand. "This ain't just for me. This is for Noley Mitchell, and Pete Richey." He glanced at Hufstedler. "It's for Pat O'Shea and all them others. It's for you too, Davey."

He walked out to the point where Hufstedler had poured the last of the powder. David heard somebody saying, "Wait till he gets in amongst the wagons." Somebody else said, "Don't wait, Texas. Get it done."

Lusk kept his own counsel. He waited, while David's lips went dry and his heart pounded. David found himself whispering, "Do it, Lusk. Do it."

Lusk could have used a pistol, but this might have alerted Bearfield too soon. He knelt over the powder and began striking a flint. In a moment David saw the blaze. He saw the black smoke rise as the flame raced along the snakelike trail the men had left.

Lusk came trotting back. "Everybody into the ravine! And everybody hold onto your horses, or by God you'll lose them!"

Someone took the brown's reins and led him down the steep bank. Lusk said, "Hold tight, Davey, because he'll jump when them wagons go up."

David knew he ought to get down and try to protect himself from the blast, but he sat transfixed, watching through blurry eyes for the tremendous explosion that was about to come.

And he watched. And he waited.

But it didn't happen.

He heard Gene Ivy shout, "It went out, Luther. Looky yonder . . . it went out."

Luther Lusk was crying, "Oh my God. We can't let them get it. We've got to blow it." He clambered up out of the ravine and went running, rifle in his hands.

David shouted, "Luther, they'll kill you out there!"

But Lusk kept running. Thirty yards out he dropped onto one knee and began firing at the wagons.

The others realized what he was trying to do. Fermin Hernandez rushed out, and Gene Ivy and Homer Gilman and some of the Yankees. They formed a line on either side of Luther Lusk, and all of them set in to firing.

Martha Townsend cried, "There goes Bearfield! He's getting away!"

Someone placed a bullet where it was wanted. David saw a flash and felt the ground tremble before he heard the thunder. He could see the chain of flashes and feel the heavy reverberations as the blasts raced from one wagon to the next. A great billow of black smoke rose up from the wagon circle, its underbelly red as it reflected the secondary explosions that followed the first great convulsions.

The brown horse panicked, jumping, squealing in terror. It was beyond David's ability to control him; he did well to hang onto the saddle. Someone grabbed the reins and threw arms around the horse's neck and held him, talking to him as he transferred his hold to the animal's ears.

The brown settled down. As the explosions stopped, David could hear someone a long way off, screaming. He could see a point of flame, moving erratically across the open ground.

"It's Bearfield," he heard Martha cry. "He's afire."

The screaming went on until Luther Lusk and a couple of the others began firing again. The flame stopped moving. It went to the ground.

"Well," said the Yankee sergeant after a minute, "he got what he came for. He just didn't expect to get it all at one time."

David looked around. He saw Martha and her father and Tom Chancellor huddled, holding onto one another.

An old debt had been paid.

The men retreated to the ravine and began making preparations to defend themselves. David thought surely the Indians would attack out of rage and frustration. Gradually they began pulling into little groups, then finally all in one large council.

They'll be coming now, he thought.

Instead, they strung out into a line and began riding off to the east. In a little while they were gone in the direction of the open plains.

A long quiet fell over the people in the ravine. They stood watching the remnants of the wagons burning in that rough circle, the smoke still drifting thick and heavy over them, obscuring the sun.

At last Luther Lusk said, "Davey, I think we've all seen enough of this place. We could make a few miles before dark catches us, if you think you're able."

David turned in the saddle, looking for Martha Townsend. He stared at her for a minute. He did not see what he had hoped he might. She and Tom Chancellor leaned to-

ether, their arms around each other. David turned again
ntil he found Owen Townsend and the Yankee sergeant.
Ie said, "We're thinkin' we'll ride on a ways south while the
ight is with us, if you folks don't have it in mind to try and
top us."

Townsend glanced at the sergeant. "I believe they have us
utnumbered."

"That," the sergeant replied flatly, "is also my belief."

The Texans began swinging onto their horses. David
ooked again at Martha Townsend. She walked to him, leav-
ng Chancellor. David moved the brown horse out away
rom the people. Martha followed him.

David reached down, and Martha took his hand. He said,
I wish I could ask you to go with us."

She nodded. "But you can't. And I couldn't go with you,
ven if you could ask."

His gaze drifted to the burned wagons. "I put you
hrough hell, and it was all for nothin'. I'm sorry."

"Don't be sorry you tried. You never had a chance from
he beginning. You Texans had lost New Mexico long before
ou ever got to our place. Nothing you could have done
vould have changed that. What you did, trying to get to
Texas with this wagon train, was just a gallant gesture,
iothing more. What you did just now, blowing it all up, was
he most gallant thing of all. I am proud now that I got to
:now you."

David's throat was tight. "Martha, I wish we could've met
ome other time, some other place. I wish there didn't have
o be this war between us." He frowned. "I thought once it
vas goin' to be a short one. But what I've seen of your peo-
le here, and what I know of ours, it's apt to run on for a
ong time."

Tears came into her eyes. "Yes, I'm afraid it will."

"But it'll be over someday. I was wonderin' . . . when it
loes, I might just find my way back over into this coun-
ry . . ."

She shook her head. "You won't, Texas. Even if you did, it
vouldn't be of any use." She glanced back toward Tom
Chancellor. "You've seen how it is."

If he hadn't already, he could see it now, in her eyes. H folded both his hands over her hand. "Then, all I can say i be happy." He leaned to kiss the tips of her fingers, and h let her go.

He turned, looking for Lusk. Fermin Hernandez wa there. Hernandez said, "I take the point, Lieutenant."

David shook his head. "You don't have to. I'll get some body else."

Hernandez smiled. "It is all right. I like it there. U front, I don't have to listen to foolish talk." He touche spurs lightly to his horse.

David looked around again for Lusk. This time he foun him. "We all ready?"

"Ready."

David grimaced as he put his hand to the burning hip wishing he could ease the throbbing. It would be hell, bu damned if it was going to stop him. He glanced back once a Martha and the others and brought his hand up in a sma salute. He said, "Let's go. It's still a long ways back t Texas."

KELTON
ON
KELTON

I was born at a place called Horse Camp on the Scharbauer Cattle Company's Five Wells Ranch in Andrews County, Texas, in 1926. My father was a cowboy there, and my grandfather was the ranch foreman. My great-grandfather had come out from East Texas about 1876 with a wagon and a string of horses to become a ranchman, but he died young, leaving four small boys to grow up as cowpunchers and bronc breakers. With all that heritage I should have become a good cowboy myself, but somehow I never did, so I decided if I could not do it I would write about it.

I studied journalism at the University of Texas and became a livestock and farm reporter in San Angelo, Texas, writing fiction as a sideline to newspaper work. I have maintained the two careers in parallel more than thirty years. My fiction has been mostly about Texas, about areas whose history and people I know from long study and long personal acquaintance. I have always believed we can learn much about ourselves by studying our history, for we are the products of all that has gone before us. All history is relevant today, because the way we live—the values we believe in—are a result of molds prepared for us by our forebears a long time ago.

I was an infantryman in World War II and married an Austrian girl, Anna, I met there shortly after the war. We raised three children, all grown now and independent, proud of their mixed heritage of the Old World on one hand and the Texas frontier on the other.

PUBLISHER'S NOTE

Elmer Kelton won the Western Heritage Award for Best Novel for his 1987 book *The Man Who Rode Midnight*.

ELMER KELTON

THE MAN WHO RODE MIDNIGHT

☐ 27713 $3.50

Bantam is pleased to offer these exciting Western adventures by ELMER KELTON, one of the great Western storytellers with a special talent for capturing the fiercely independent spirit of the West:

☐	25658	AFTER THE BUGLES	$2.95
☐	27351	HORSEHEAD CROSSING	$2.95
☐	27119	LLANO RIVER	$2.95
☐	27218	MANHUNTERS	$2.95
☐	27620	HANGING JUDGE	$2.95
☐	27467	WAGONTONGUE	$2.95
☐	25629	BOWIE'S MINE	$2.95
☐	26999	MASSACRE AT GOLIAD	$2.95
☐	25651	EYES OF THE HAWK	$2.95
☐	26042	JOE PEPPER	$2.95

"An American original."
—*The New York Times Book Review*

ELMORE LEONARD

For rugged stories of the American frontier, there is no writer quite like Elmore Leonard. Pick up these exciting westerns at your local bookstore—or use the handy coupon below for ordering.

☐ **ESCAPE FROM FIVE SHADOWS** (27202 • $2.95)

☐ **FORTY LASHES LESS ONE** (27625 • $2.95)

☐ **THE BOUNTY HUNTERS** (27099 • $2.95)

☐ **GUNSIGHTS** (27337 • $2.95)

☐ **VALDEZ IS COMING** (27098 • $2.95)

☐ **LAST STAND AT SABER RIVER** (27097 • $2.95)

☐ **THE LAW AT RANDADO** (27201 • $2.95)